MW01229116

Chasing the Wicked

A captivating crime thriller

D.J. Maughan

Hulyeseg Publishing

For you, Momma. Thank you for your love and support. You could have sent me to bed; instead, you played air hockey with me Christmas morning at three a.m.. I love you!

Chapter One

Peter

February 14, 2001 – Budapest

Peter's mother warned him that women are complicated. But an abducted woman can be downright intolerable. Especially if you're the one who kidnapped her. She doesn't believe you when you tell her it was for her own good. To save her life. Covering her mouth, throwing her in a van, and doing all this while you wear a ski mask instills a healthy degree of skepticism.

"Look, I know we didn't exactly get started in an ideal way. But you have to trust me. Your life was in danger."

Andrassy Peter sits on the van's bench seat next to Lili, the television reporter he had abducted moments ago. She eyes him suspiciously, one hand still on the door handle. Ready to spring from the vehicle at any moment.

"Who are you?"

"I told you; my name is Andrassy Peter. The guy driving is Lantos Tamás. We took you to protect you. To prevent your abduction."

"By who?"

"That's not easy to explain."

"Try me."

"A man by the name of Toth József."

"Who's that? Is that who killed Agnes?"

Peter's face turns hard, and he stares into her eyes. "Someone killed Agnes?"

Lili frowns. "You know her?"

"Yes."

"How?"

Peter shakes his head and grabs her arm. "Tell me what happened to her."

"I don't know. My news director told me. He fired me because of my interview with her. He said she was killed and that my interview caused it."

Peter turns away from Lili and looks at Tom before returning his gaze to her. "What about Renata?"

"You know her too?"

"Yes."

"How?"

He shakes his head. "I'll tell you later." He tightens his grip on her arm. "If Agnes was killed, Renata's in danger too. Did your news director say anything about her?"

"No."

"Hey, Peter," Tom says from behind the wheel.

"Yeah."

"I think we're being followed." Peter puts his arm over the seat and looks back. He sees a set of headlights far enough behind to not appear obvious but close enough to stay within following distance. "They've been behind us since Aquincum."

Peter reaches over, picks up the ski mask, and places it back over his head.

"What's going on?" Lili asks. "Why are you wearing a mask? Are you going to tell me anything?"

Peter ignores her and climbs into the front seat next to Tom. "I have to wear a mask. It's important that certain people don't recognize me."

Lili frowns and looks at Tom, who nods before she turns back to Peter. "Are you wanted or something?"

Peter has his arm over the bench seat, looking back, watching the car behind them. "Kind of. Certain people think I'm in America. For the time being, I want to keep it that way." He turns and looks at Tom. "How are your driving skills?"

"Better if I'm driving slowly on a driveway. If you want me to do anything fancy, I'd probably kill all of us in the process."

"We're going to have to switch seats then. After we ascend the hill, put it in neutral."

Peter turns back and looks at Lili through his ski mask. "Toth József is the director of the Hungarian National Police. He's also responsible for all the young girls missing throughout Budapest. He's the one who had Renata abducted. We have a history, and I don't want him to know I'm back in Hungary." He turns back, looks through the windshield, then asks, "You ready?" to Tom.

"For what?" the old man replies.

"To switch seats."

"While I'm driving?"

"Yes."

"How?"

"Put the car in neutral and get out of the way so I can drive."

"Are you crazy? We're coming up on Budakezi. Can't we just pull off there?"

"No. That's where I'm going to lose him."

Tom raises his voice and points to the line of cars in the opposite lane. "Don't you see all those cars? We're going to lose control and smash into one."

"No, we aren't. I'll keep my hand on the wheel the whole time. You just need to get out of the way."

Tom shakes his head but knows better than to argue. He pops the stick into neutral and leverages his body forward, pushing against the wheel. He seems frozen in place, unsure what to do next. Peter grabs him and pulls him over the top of himself. Tom falls to the side, bumping into the gear shift. His arms and legs splay out. Peter slides underneath him, losing grip of the steering wheel. Headlights flash as they cross the center lane, angling toward oncoming traffic. Lili screams and covers her eyes as Peter grabs and turns the wheel, throwing his unbelted passengers against the passenger doors. Never releasing her grip on the door handle, Lili accidentally releases the catch in the hold as she falls into it. The door swings open, and she's suddenly falling into the cold night air. Her fall is interrupted when the pocket of her jacket snags on the arm of the seat.

A chorus of horns blares as Peter throws the van in gear and settles behind the wheel.

"Get that door closed," he says to Lili.

Lili reaches over but doesn't have the strength to pull it closed against the harsh wind. Peter looks at Tom, his legs sprawled over the seat beside him. "She's going to need help."

Tom looks at him, out of breath. "I don't remember you telling me about this part when you invited me to come along." He has to yell in order for his voice to be heard over the wind blustering through the open door. He pushes up to a seated position, then swings a leg over the back of the seat. As fast as a man can at his advanced age, Tom climbs over the back and crashes down next to Lili, crying out in pain.

"You okay?" Peter shouts.

"No." Tom groans. He rolls over next to Lili and leans out the door. He puts his hand over Lili's, and together they gather enough leverage to close the door. Tom falls back onto the seat with a huff.

"Good job," Peter says, watching them in the rearview mirror.

Tom lays on the seat and extends his middle finger. Lili doesn't see it; she's too busy pushing her long blond hair out of her face.

"Put your seat belts on," Peter tells them, unable to hide the smile. "It's about to get crazy."

"*That* wasn't crazy?" Tom asks, coughing and reaching for his belt.

Since grabbing Lili outside her office in northern Buda, they had driven through half the city, then up the Buda Hills and around the backside. Now, the line of trees is beginning to give way to buildings. Peter looks in his rearview mirror. The car's closer, but he still can't make out anything about the driver. He wonders if it's the same person who killed Detective Kovacs.

In front of their van is a truck full of pigs. Pigs are everywhere in Hungary. Centuries ago, when the Turks conquered Hungary and heavily taxed the people, Hungarians figured out Turks wouldn't take their pigs. Hungarians began raising pigs by the thousands. It's not unusual now to see a truck full of pigs crammed into the back of a truck like this one.

This isn't Peter's first time driving through Budakeszi. If his memory is correct, they'll be soon coming up on a traffic light. He slows and stays close behind the pig truck. The white sedan remains back. Keeping an irregular amount of space between them. The light turns yellow, and the truck slams on its brakes. Peter ignores the truck and hits the gas, veering into oncoming traffic. The cars see him and slam on their brakes, horns blaring. Peter turns back to the truck, clipping it as he goes by. There's a screeching sound of metal as he connects with the side of the truck.

The trailing sedan accelerates behind Peter. But as it does, a spooked pig lets its bowels loose off the side of the truck. The solid waste shoots outward and hits the windshield of the sedan. The driver, no longer able to see, overcorrects and slams into the pig truck.

Peter watches in his rearview mirror, turning his attention back to the traffic in front of him just in time. He swerves, narrowly missing the line of cars coming toward him. He accelerates through the intersection, drives two blocks, then takes a left into a neighborhood. He cuts his lights and drives through narrow streets, turning left sometimes and right others. Feeling safe they're no longer being followed, he pulls to the side of the road and turns off the van. He removes his mask and grins at Tom. Tom shakes his head and rolls his eyes.

"Okay, that was pretty impressive, I'll give you that. I take back flipping you off."

Peter laughs and looks at Lili. Her eyes are large, and she's breathing rapidly, her hand braced on the seat before her.

"You okay?" Peter asks.

She nods, swallowing. "I thought we were dead."

Peter shakes his head. "Oh, come on. We had at least...six inches." He laughs at the expression on her face. "We'll sit tight for a while. Ensure the sedan has lost us, then continue."

"To where?

"Tatabánya."

"Tatabánya? Why there?"

"Exactly. Nobody will be looking for you there. Also, Tom has a sister there. She'll keep you safe. And from what I hear, she's a heck of a cook."

Lili turns and looks at Tom, and he shrugs.

"So I can't go home?" she asks Peter.

"Not unless you want to end up like Agnes. That person in the sedan was sent to abduct you. If they got you, you'd end up dead or in another nasty spot."

"Like what?"

"Like sold as a slave, probably in another country."

"Is that where all these girls are going? Is that what would have happened to Renata?"

"I think so. I don't have all the details yet, but I know enough."

She frowns, and Peter can see the concern in her eyes.

"Renata was fortunate to get away. To my knowledge, she's the only one who has."

"And this is all being done by Director Toth, the head of the Hungarian National Police?"

"Yep. In fact, I bet you've seen him before."

"Yes, I have. He was on TV, talking about Nagy Béla, the newspaper columnist who went missing. Do you think Toth was responsible?"

"I do."

She nods and looks out the window, processing the information. "I knew Béla. We were conversing about the abductions."

"Well...that's another reason Toth would be after you."

She turns back to Peter now, her face grave. "He's a powerful man. He controls the police. How are you going to stop him?" She sees intensity in his eyes when he replies.

"I've got an idea. And you're going to help me."

Chapter Two

Director Toth

Past – Budapest

"Papa, what are these?"

My father stands beside me but doesn't notice as I point at the orange-colored balls on the shelf. He's talking with another man, keeping his voice low. They know each other. They work in the factory together.

"I agree," my father says, "but at what cost?"

The man is much smaller than Father, and there is something unnatural about his face. Is it his eyes? They look too close together. Maybe it's his nose. It looks like a beak. I don't like him. I want to leave.

"So what are you saying? You don't like the communist ideology? You think we should be like the West?"

"Not at all," my father says. "It's just that we've lost so much territory since the Great War. We Hungarians don't govern ourselves. Nagy and Rákosi are puppets. The Russians need to leave and give Hungary back to the Hungarians. We can remain allies. Remain communist. But we should decide." My father turns and points to the orange balls. "We only have oranges once a year for Christmas. Before the war, we had them all the time. It's an example of what we've lost."

So that's what they're called. Oranges. I wonder what they are. What do you do with them? Are they a toy? A ball used in a game?

My father and the man continue talking as I tug on my father's arm. He doesn't even look at me. His whisper intense. Finally, they finish, and my father turns to me. He motions to the shop clerk, who hands him three oranges. Father gives him some forint, and we walk out of the shop. As we walk toward home in the dark, Father hands me an orange.

"József, this one is yours."

I take it from him and examine it.

"How do I play with it?"

He laughs and reaches down, tousling my hair. "You eat it. You peel off that hard skin and reveal the sweetest fruit you've ever tasted. We'll save them until tomorrow. Each of us can have one: me, you, and your mother."

We arrive home, and Mother welcomes us. She's prepared fish soup. The next day, Christmas Day, after dinner, Father finally tells me it's time. I haven't let my orange out of sight since we came home. I've wanted so badly to slice it open and taste the sweetness. Last night, after Mother and Father fell asleep, I almost gave in. I scratched the surface with my finger. I smelled the sweet, tangy scent. I ran my tongue along the cut surface, hoping to get a taste. I was disappointed. It didn't taste sweet. It was bitter. There might have been a sweet tinge, but that faded to tart. Had Father lied to me? Was he playing a trick? After that taste, my craving subsided. I was able to put the orange aside and sleep. When I woke and saw the orange sitting on the table, my curiosity burned. I had to know.

"József, come here." My father commands.

My mother smiles at me, her orange in her hand.

My father, with me watching, pierces the skin of his orange. "You cut the skin, then peel it. Like this." He takes off chunks of peel, revealing a white surface below. Once all the skin is removed, he tears it open. I stare down at it. He begins to separate the orange into sections. The sweet smell of citrus fills the air. He wasn't lying. Was he? I feel a jolt of panic. Maybe he likes the taste, but I won't. It wouldn't be the first time. He let me sip his wine after dinner a few months back. He laughed at my grimace as I tried to swallow.

"Now it's your turn."

He hands me the knife, and I pierce the skin and peel it back. Before long, I have my pieces of orange arranged on the plate. My mother and father smile, sensing my excitement.

"Go ahead," he tells me, motioning with his hand. "Eat it." He laughs at my nervousness.

A loud knock startles us, and I nearly knock over my plate. Father goes to the door and swings it wide. He steps back as two men in green uniforms enter.

"Toth Imre?" the older man asks, staring at my father.

"Yes."

He looks at the other man and nods. They come forward and grab my father. Father pushes them away.

"What is this? Who are you?"

The older man removes a large stick from his belt and swings it at Father. Mother and I watch in horror as he cries out in pain. The man raises the stick and hits him repeatedly until Father is no longer resisting.

Mother sits at the table sobbing, holding her hand to her lips.

Once subdued, they grab Father and pull him out the door.

Mother stands and goes to the opening. I follow, warily hiding behind her. We see no trace of them as we look out on the street. Only footprints remain in the freshly fallen snow.

It's been two weeks since my father was taken from our home. There's been no sign of him. No news. Each night, I sit listening, playing on the floor with my blocks or marbles. Hoping I'll hear the heavy thud of his boots on our porch. I want him to come home. I need him. Mother needs him. She's withdrawn. It's like she's dead inside. She sits staring out the window every night after work. At first, I thought she was waiting for him to come home. Hoping to be the first to see him. But it's more than that. Her stare is vacant. Her eyes never focus.

I try to talk to her, to get her to eat something. She's not interested. She goes to work and comes home. Never speaking. Does she know where he is? Is he not coming back?

As I sit, moving blocks around, pretending to play, I watch her. She's sitting there, staring off. Finally, she looks at me. There's no familiarity in her eyes. It's as if she doesn't know me. Like I'm a stranger. She stands and walks to the bathroom. She closes the door. I can hear her shuffling around. I wait to hear the toilet flush, but it never does. I sit on my knees on the floor, watching for movement. Listening. There's no sound. What is she doing?

I can't wait any longer. I stand and walk down the hall to the bathroom. I need to go really bad. I might not make it in time. I bang on the door.

"Mother? I need to go."

No answer.

"Mother? Please, I need to go."

Still nothing.

I try the doorknob, and I'm surprised when it turns. I open the door and stop. My eyes are drawn to the crimson line running from the tub along the floor. It's so long it nearly reaches the door, spanning the entire bathroom. I raise my gaze to the tub and see her. She's in the bathtub with all her clothes on and no water. Her left arm hangs off the ledge. I tiptoe near her, careful not to touch any of the blood.

"Mother?" I whisper, panic rising.

She doesn't respond.

I pass the toilet and reach her. Her head is on the back of the tub, her other arm by her side, her wrist turned upward. Blood covers her hands and wrists. Her eyes are open but vacant. Her face is ashen.

"Mother?" I whisper.

Nothing. Only the irregular bursts of my own breathing.

Chapter Three

Director Toth

Present

I sit, drumming my fingers on the desk and looking at the clock on the wall. Tardiness is something I don't tolerate, and Gyula knows it. He's making me wait. He seems to have forgotten who I am. What our relationship is. Maybe it's time I remind him. A knock sounds at the door, and my eyes dart over.

"Come," I bark.

I expect him to cower as he enters. He's a little man, much shorter than myself. I'm anticipating groveling mixed with apologies. Instead, he saunters in, barely aware of the time. Rage boils within me, and I nearly explode before a thought occurs to me: Does he know? Is that why he's not afraid? Has he learned something? The idea replaces my anger with anxiety. I sit scrutinizing him as he walks closer. He carries a folder in his hand. I wonder what it contains. If he knows, has he told anyone?

He reaches the chair across the desk but doesn't sit. He waits for an invitation.

"Sit," I command, waving an upturned hand.

He sidesteps around the chair and sits, peering at me through the magnifying glasses he calls spectacles. We stare at each other. Neither speaking.

"Well...," I finally say.

"The divers searched the entire river near Margit Island. Nothing. He's not there."

This is expected. After drowning Béla, the columnist from the *Magyar Hírlap*, I had his body found and moved. It's an incredible advantage when you know where the police will look before they do. When Gyula told me he was bringing in divers, I knew Béla would need to be exhumed from his watery grave.

"So what does that mean? Where is he?"

Gyula shakes his head and looks away, pulling at his lip. "I'm not sure."

"Could he still be alive?"

"No, he's dead. And I'm confident he died there on the island. The killer moved the body. To where? I don't know."

"What makes you so sure?"

He turns back to me. His beady, little eyes stare at me through inches of glass. "I don't have any evidence, if that's what you mean. Just a feeling. A hunch."

I can feel myself relax. But I don't show it. At least, I hope I don't. "So, what now?"

He shrugs. "Without a body, this remains a missing-persons case. We've searched his house and office. We've interviewed everyone close to him: friends, family, colleagues. The guy is squeaky clean. There's no motive other than the stories about the missing girls."

"They're related? The missing girls and his disappearance?"

He nods. "Without a doubt."

There's one more thing I want to ask. One other item I need from him. But I don't want to say it. I want him to volunteer the information. We stare at each other before I finally give in.

"So that's it? Nothing else to investigate?"

He shakes his head. "Not right now."

"What about the internet café? You said you might know who sent the emails to him. This concerned citizen?"

He pauses. *What's going on in his mind?*

"That's become interesting."

"How so?"

"The girl working in the café at the time of the computer usage is gone."

"Gone? What do you mean gone?"

"Vanished. Nobody's seen her. She stopped coming to work and seems to have disappeared. Poof. Nobody's heard from her. Not her family or friends. Nobody at work."

I frown and strum my fingers on the desk. "Is it related?"

He cocks his head to the side. "I have to assume it is."

"So that's it? Without the girl, we have nothing else we can investigate?"

He shrugs. "Oh, we know what computer was used. But the email account was a dummy account. The person set up and used the account to communicate with Béla. Nothing else. It's a dead end without the girl."

I lean back and steeple my fingers. "Didn't you tell me there was a video camera?"

"Yes. But the tape used for recording is recorded over each night. By the time we got to it, five new days were recorded over the top."

I sigh and come forward. I want him out of my office. "Well...okay then. Let me know if anything new comes up."

He stands and moves toward the door, taking the hint. When he opens it, he stops and turns around. He looks at me, and our eyes lock. *What's he thinking?* He says nothing and closes the door behind him. I had planned to pick up the phone and make a call, but his behavior stops me. *What was that?* Gyula would never be accused of being friendly. In fact, several detectives over the years have asked to be transferred away from him. But he's always been respectful of me. This was different. He had an air of contempt. I sit with my chin on my fists before finally raising the phone to my ear and dialing.

"Sir?"

"What have you done?" I ask.

"What do you mean?"

"You know what I mean. What happened to the girl?"

A pause on the other end of the phone. "We'll find her."

"You mean, you don't have her?"

Another pause.

"Sir, you know Renata got away."

"I'm not talking about Renata. I'm talking about the girl who works at the internet café. You took her without telling me."

The voice is uncertain. "No, we didn't. We were waiting for you. You told me not to act yet, and I didn't." I can't believe what I'm hearing. If we didn't take her, who did? Where is she?

"Sir?"

"Yes."

"She's gone?"

"Yes. We've got to find her. Look into her family, friends, any possible link to where she might have gone."

"You've got it, Boss."

We hang up, and I stand from my desk and walk to the window. I look down on Budapest and the scores of people milling around. I thought it was unfortunate when Renata went missing. More a nuisance. But this is troublesome. Renata knows nothing about me or anyone else. She can't identify a soul connected. This girl is different. She could.

Chapter Four

Zsuzsa

I poke around the corner and see Kata frowning at the computer screen.

"Is it that bad?"

She jumps in her seat. I wasn't trying to startle her. "Oh, Zsuzsa. You scared me."

"I'm sorry," I say as I enter the office and sit opposite her. "I guess I have that effect on people. Margit just told me one of the new girls is scared of me."

"Really?"

"Apparently."

"Who?"

"Judit. I think that's her name."

Kata waves a hand. "Oh, she's timid. That's her, not you. I wouldn't worry about that." She goes back to looking at the computer screen.

"So, why were you frowning at the monitor?"

"Was I?"

"It looked like it."

"Well, I should be smiling."

"Oh?"

"Yeah, it looks like your boyfriend is a genius. Since we started doing his idea, we've added five hundred people to our database, and we're in the midst of the best sales month we've ever had."

I stand and go to her, wrapping an arm around her shoulder. "That's so great. I'm so happy." She stands, and we hug. "He'll be so pleased to hear it."

"When do you see him next?"

"Tonight. Looks like we've got something to celebrate."

Five hours later, I walk hand in hand with Gabor as the hostess shows us to our table. Gabor requested a seat near the window and, like always, his choice was perfect. He smiles as he watches me look past him at the view. The hostess points to our table, and he lets me take the seat opposite the window. Once settled, he asks, "Have you ever been here?"

I don't immediately answer. I'm in awe of the view. "What?"

"Visegrád, have you ever been here?"

"Once. When I was a little girl. It's been a long time."

The sun's setting over the hills on the other side of the river. It's beautiful now, but I wish we were here in the spring. I imagine it's breathtaking.

He turns around and points. "That side of the Danube is Slovakia. Visegrád was the royal seat of Hungary way back in the thirteen hundreds. You remember that castle we saw as we walked up here? That was the king's palace. The throne, crown jewels, everything used to be here."

I look at him and smile. "Is there anything you don't know?"

He laughs. "Maybe I just bring you places like this to impress you."

"Well, it's working. I'm more than impressed. I'm starting to think you might be perfect."

He looks me in the eye, and I can see he wants to say something but hesitates. The server reaches our table and welcomes us. He hands us both menus, and we pick a wine. As we review our dinner menu, I ask Gabor for a recommendation.

"Hmm. What are you in the mood for?"

"Give me some options."

He scrutinizes the menu. "Well, I'd recommend the quinoa pasta with vegetables if you want something lighter. If you want something heartier, I'd go with the wild boar and ask for it with spicy potatoes. They're delicious. Oh, and don't skip over the fruit soup. I love it."

"How often do you come here?"

He smiles. "Once I've dated a girl at least three times, I bring her here. So...a lot."

"Oh, well...I guess I shouldn't feel that flattered then."

"I was kidding."

Our server returns, and I order the quinoa and the fruit soup. He orders the wild boar.

"You've got to try it. I'll share a little with you."

"Sounds good."

We fall silent, and I go back to looking out the window. We make eye contact, and he smiles. I can see there's still something there. Something he wants to say, but he's hesitant.

"What is it, Gabor?"

"What?"

"What's on your mind?"

"I've thought a lot about what you said to me the other night."

"In my apartment?"

"Yeah."

"What, exactly?"

"Lots of things. About your former employer, Andras. About the girls going missing. About Peter."

"Peter's gone."

"I know. But I do feel some jealousy. I know you care about him."

I pick up my wine glass and look at him over the top.

"I know you knew him before you knew me. But I—"

"What? You want me to forget him?"

"Maybe."

A chink in the armor. How can he be jealous of a man thousands of miles away who I'll never see again? "Well, that's not going to happen. Should I ask you to forget your ex-wife?"

The server arrives with our food. He places mine before me, but I've lost my appetite. Gabor has disappointed me. After the server leaves, Gabor grabs my hand across the table.

"I'm sorry. That was stupid. I don't know what came over me. I won't mention Peter again. Please forget I said that."

I force a smile and squeeze his hand. "I forgive you."

We begin to eat, and our conversation turns lighter. We discuss work, the weather, and places we'd like to travel. It's nice, and I've almost put our earlier flare-up out of my mind when he says, "Zsuzsa, I'm sorry, but there's one more thing I need to say."

I put down my fork and shoot him a look.

"There's something I want you to do for me."

This surprises me. "What?"

"I want you to leave that woman alone. The one in Újpest. She's been through enough already, losing her daughter. Don't make it worse. Let her be."

I stare at him, a jumble of thoughts running through my head. I can see why he would say this, but what about the missing girls? The woman may know who's responsible. With that knowledge, we might be able to stop them.

"It's not just her I worry about. It's you. Somebody was following you the other night. You don't know who else might be watching. If you go back to see her, you'll endanger her and yourself. Is it worth that?"

I look away, and he grabs my hand again.

"Just think about it. Okay?"

I look into his eyes and nod, fighting to hide my annoyance. What does he know about the situation? He only knows what I've told him. I stood to the side while Andras abducted women I knew, women I worked with. If I can do something to prevent that from happening, it's my obligation, regardless of the danger.

Chapter Five

Peter

Peter parks the white Volkswagen van at the Westend Mall's parking center, walks through the mall, and enters the north train station. He climbs aboard a northbound subway train toward Újpest. After several stops, he exits and walks to Renata and Agnes's apartment building. Since hearing Lili talk about Agnes's murder, Peter hasn't gotten Renata out of his head. Was she killed too? Doubtful. If so, wouldn't Lili have known? Does she realize the danger she's in?

He stops as he nears the apartment building and waits. There's no indication a murder took place here a few days ago. No yellow caution tape outside. He examines each surrounding building but sees nobody watching the apartment. He's surprised there are no police vehicles parked at the curb. If Renata were here, wouldn't they be watching her? Knowing he's taking a risk, but deciding he has no choice, he crosses the road and enters the building, keeping his head low. He climbs the steps to the girls' apartment and slows when he reaches the floor landing. He pokes his head around the corner of the stairwell. Everything looks normal, except the yellow police tape blocking the apartment. A *Belépni tilos* (Do not enter) sign is plastered to the door.

Peter climbs one floor higher and surveys the area before returning. He can't see any signs of the apartment being watched. If the tape is on the door, Renata must not be staying here. But if she's not, where is she? Maybe the answer is inside the apartment.

An idea surfaces, and he walks to the neighboring door and rings the bell. No answer. He rings again. Still nothing. He listens closely and can't hear any dogs on the other side. Using the skill he picked up from a common thief years ago in New York City, he pops the lock on the door and enters. The apartment is small and dark. He walks to the back of the living space, his head on a swivel, making sure he isn't surprised.

He reaches the back windows and pulls one open. He leans out and sees his memory is correct. The girls have a small landing outside one of the two apartment windows. He looks around, making sure nobody is watching, then climbs out onto the ledge. He avoids looking down, knowing if he does, he might back out. He takes a breath and jumps. He catches the railing and feels his hands slip. He squeezes harder and pulls with all his might. He brings himself high enough to reach a foot on the landing and stand. With his feet on solid ground and his hands around the metal, he allows himself to look down at the six levels below. If he had missed, he would have been killed. He takes a breath and pulls on the window. Luckily, it slides open. He enters the apartment and closes the window behind him.

He's in the kitchen. Everything looks similar to the way it had weeks ago. He exits the kitchen and walks down the hallway. He enters the bedroom shared by the two girls and looks around. The room looks lived in, with clothing on the floor and unmade bedding. He walks to Renata's bed and pulls up the mattress. The diary is still there. He grabs it, pops the lock, and scrolls to the back. He can remember reading the name of the university she attends in one of her passages. As he scans the dates of each entry, he hears something at the front of the apartment. He stands, goes to the bedroom door, and looks down the hallway. Even from this distance, he can see the turn of the doorknob. Somebody's coming.

Peter steps back behind the bedroom door and looks around. The room is small with nowhere to hide. Is it the police? Maybe Renata? He leans forward and presses his eye between the doorframe and door. It's a man. He's young, perhaps eighteen. He's coming straight for the bedroom. Peter slides the diary into his coat pocket, steps back against the wall behind the door, and waits. The boy pushes open the door and enters the room. He looks around, walks to Agnes's bed, and raises the mattress. He scans the surface, then drops it. He walks to the other bed and repeats the process. When he drops the mattress, Peter pushes the door forward, slamming it shut. The boy jumps and whirls around. Peter stands with his gun pointed at the boy.

"Who are you?" Peter demands.

The boy stands there in shock, hands raised.

"Who are you?" Peter tries again.

"Dominic."

Peter glares at him. "Renata told you to come, didn't she?"

The boy's eyes go wide, but he says nothing.

"Didn't she?"

He winces and nods. "How do you know?"

"Where is she?"

He stares back at Peter, saying nothing.

"Is she okay?"

Again, nothing.

"Look, kid, I'm not here to hurt her. I'm Peter. I found her in Ukraine and brought her home."

The boy relaxes. "Peter? She told me about you."

Peter lowers the gun and pulls the diary from his jacket. "Looking for this?"

He nods. "Renata wanted me to get it."

Peter walks over and moves to hand it to him but stops. "I'll give it to you on one condition."

"What?"

"You never come back here. No matter what. I don't care what Renata says. Promise me you'll never return. If they catch you, they'll kill you. But they won't do it like Agnes; they'll torture you first. They'll make you tell them where Renata is. Do you understand me?"

The boy nods, and Peter hands him the diary.

"Where's Renata? Is she staying with you?"

He shakes his head.

"Good. Wait a second." He indicates with his hand that the boy should return the diary to him. He opens it and flips to the back page. He pulls out the pen and writes his number. "If anything happens, you tell Renata to call me. If she thinks someone knows where she is, you tell her to call this number. Got it?"

The boy nods. Peter hands the diary back to him but locks it first. What's written inside is personal, and he doesn't want Dominic to be tempted to read it.

Two hours later, Peter sits in the van across the street from Zsuzsa's apartment building. He knows he shouldn't, but the desire to see her, even from afar, wins out. He tells himself he's not going to approach. He just wants a glimpse. Not an hour goes by when he doesn't think about her.

He looks down at his watch. It's ten thirty. If she was working tonight, she'd be coming home soon. He sits, feeling the anticipation grow. He's missed her, and although he won't be able to approach her, the thought of seeing her excites him.

Another twenty minutes go by, and he nearly gives up when a red BMW pulls up to the front of the building. A fit-looking man exits the driver's seat, walks to the passenger side, and opens the door. He reaches in and grasps a hand. Peter doesn't need to see the long blond hair to know. He feels his heart sink as he watches Zsuzsa exit the car. He tries to look away but can't as they walk to the building, hand in hand.

Peter anxiously looks on as they reach the front door, and she turns back to the man. There they stand, facing each other. The man says something, and Zsuzsa smiles up at him. He leans forward, and Peter feels himself inhale as Zsuzsa welcomes his kiss. Peter looks away, feeling sick. He looks down; the hurt is crippling. He longs to start the car and drive away but knows he can't bring attention to himself. All he can do is sit, occasionally looking up, brokenhearted as the woman he loves kisses another man.

Chapter Six

Detective Szabo

I sit looking out the interior window of my office watching each member of my team. Which one is it? Varga? No, she's a woman. How could it be her? She wouldn't be involved in trafficking other women. Plus, they were going to abduct her. If it was her, wouldn't they have left her alone in the club when we used her as bait? Katona? No, he's too new to the team. He joined after Kovacs was killed and Peter was arrested. He wouldn't have been privy to any information during the months trafficking raged in the city. Although, he was on the bridge that day when Kovacs died. He was a uniformed cop then before Toth promoted him to detective. Is there a way he could have gathered the information without being on the team?

My eyes lock on Farkas. It's got to be him. He's male, has been here the whole time, and he's just too good. He's the kind of coworker you love but hate. He's always on time, does what is asked of him, speaks when spoken to, and doesn't get involved in politics or interoffice gossip. He's a perfect cop. Maybe too perfect.

I stand and take three steps to the filing cabinet on the opposite wall. I pull out his employee file and walk back to my desk. I open it, but I'm unsure what I'm looking for. There's a photo of Farkas in the front. He's younger, wearing an officer's uniform, his hair short. I scan the background information. Born in Dunaújváros, also known as "Stalin City" during communism. He has two siblings. His father is a construction worker. His mother is a schoolteacher. Both siblings are older sisters. He's the baby. Parents are still living. One sister lives in Székesfehérvár, the other in Csepel. He's unmarried. He served four years in the military before joining the academy and becoming a cop. His test scores are incredibly high. Higher than any I've ever seen.

I look up from the file, lean back, and stare at the back of his head. What could be the connection between him and the traffickers? How would he have met them? School? The military? I get an idea and walk out to the bullpen.

"Hey, does anyone know where the file is for Dobo Andras?"

Varga's on the phone; she looks at me and holds up a finger. Katona gives me a blank look. Farkas leans across his desk and rifles through an organized stack of binders. He pulls one and hands it to me. "Here you go."

"Thanks. How about Agoston, the club manager?"

"Yeah, I've got that one too."

He pulls it from his stack and hands it to me. I lean forward and scrutinize the pile. It's perfectly arranged, even alphabetized.

"What are you working on, Boss?" Katona asks. "Anything I can help with?" He's leaning back in his chair, chewing on a pen.

"No, just gathering a little background information on these two."

I walk back to my office and open Andras's file. When I sit down, I notice Farkas is still watching me. I stare back at him until he looks away. I turn my attention to the file. Andras also served in the military. But they wouldn't have overlapped. Andras was a lot older. I check the education line—different schools. Birthplaces are different also. There's nothing obviously linking the two of them. I put the file aside and pick up Agoston's.

He was never in the military. Curious, since it's mandatory. He got out of it on some bogus health condition. He attended a different university. Birthplace was different, too—no apparent link between them.

I lean back in my chair, exhale, and look at the ceiling. Something is missing, but what? I feel my frustration grow and decide to take a walk. I need a sounding board, someone I can talk to. But who? Maybe it's time I include the director in this. I haven't told him what Peter had said. If anyone could do something to help root out the mole, it would be him. Maybe it's time I trust him. I walk down the hall to his office and stop at his secretary's desk.

"Detective Szabo, how can I help you?"

"Hi, Erzsi, is the director in?"

She frowns and shakes her head.

"No, sorry. He's gone to lunch with the prosecutor general. He'll be back in a couple hours. But he does have a pretty busy day. Do you have something urgent?"

"No, it's okay. I just wanted to run something past him. Maybe tomorrow."

She looks at the calendar. "He's free at nine-thirty. Should I pencil you in?"

I open my mouth to respond but stop. Before I was in this role, as a detective on the force, I liked the director. He was always friendly and easy to talk to. Now, he's anything but. He's constantly riding me for information and has very little patience. The thought of voluntarily signing up for face-to-face time with the guy makes me rethink my strategy.

"You know, on second thought, don't worry about it. It's not important."

"You sure?"

"Yeah. Thanks, though."

We smile at each other, and I walk away. I can't find a better place to go, so I head into the bathroom. Rákosi Gyula, head of the major-crimes unit, stands at one of the urinals. I notice, with annoyance, that he's taken the taller urinal. Why would he take that one when he's barely tall enough to reach it? He looks up at me as I take the urinal beside him, bending my knees and dropping into a quarter squat.

"Hi, Gyula."

The little man grunts a greeting.

"I've been meaning to ask you, how's it going with that newspaper-reporter case? Has he been found yet?"

"No," he says and zips up his pants, turning away and heading to the sink.

"Do you think he's dead?"

He looks at me. "I don't spend my time speculating about cases." He rotates back to the sink and turns on the water.

"I only ask because it might be related to the trafficking in the city."

"It is related."

"It is?"

He glares at me.

"How do you know?"

"He was writing articles about missing girls, then he went missing. Doesn't take Sherlock Holmes to put that one together."

I finish and zip up my pants. "Maybe we should be working together on this?"

"Nope."

"Why not? Seems like our cases overlap."

He finishes at the sink and steps back. "Do you know who's doing the trafficking?"

"No."

He shrugs and turns toward the door. "Until you do, we have nothing to talk about."

Gyula starts to open the door, but I lean over and push it closed. "Someone on my team is working with the traffickers."

He looks up at me, and I seem to have his attention for the first time. "Who?"

"I'm not sure."

"How do you know?"

I can't tell him Peter told me.

"The traffickers are always one step ahead. They knew Kovacs was going to Ukraine before he did. They knew we were coming to Slovenia."

He reaches back for the door. "I'd say, before you do anything else, you better find out who it is."

Chapter Seven

Renata

"What do you think?"

I'm looking in the mirror and can hardly recognize the girl looking back at me. Zoe stands to the side, hand on her hip.

"You know what would be perfect?" she asks.

"What?"

"Hold on."

She leaves the room, and I can hear her opening a door in the hallway. She comes back with a black beret in her hand. "Turn around." She places the hat on my head, sloping it to the side. "Perfect."

I turn back to the mirror and step back. I've completely changed my look. I've traded my cute skirts and dresses for black army boots, coveralls, a black T-shirt, a jacket, and a beret. Even my hair is jet black. It's shorter too, barely below my ears. I pierced my septum and ran a black ring through my nose to complete the look.

"You look so different," Zoe tells me.

"You think?"

"Oh, yeah."

"Do you think anyone will recognize me?"

"Let's find out."

"How?"

"Let's go to the school. See if anyone knows you."

Panic rises in my chest. My mind fades back to waking up in that room in Ukraine. The IV connected to my arm—the three other girls in beds. My leg handcuffed to the bed frame.

"No!"

She jumps at my reaction, then looks me in the eye and puts her hand on my shoulder. She's so much like Agnes. "We need to test it. You can't stay in this apartment forever. We have to go somewhere where people know you. See if they recognize you."

I turn away and shake my head. "Not the school. If they know I'm enrolled there..."

"Do you have a better idea?"

I sit down on the bed and think. "What about the McDonald's?"

"What about it?"

"People from the school are always going there after class. What if we just wait there? See if we recognize anyone?"

An hour later, we sit in the McDonald's at Móricz Zsigmond Square, sipping drinks and sharing french fries, when a crowd of classmates come walking in. Zoe looks at me, and I hold her gaze. She stands and waves to them, two girls and a boy.

"Hey, Krisztina," she calls to the nearest girl.

The girl smiles and comes over. They kiss each other on the cheeks, as is customary.

When they part, Krisztina asks, "Zoe, where were you today?"

She holds her stomach. "Sick."

Krisztina points to the fries and laughs. "I don't think those are going to help."

Zoe smiles and gives her a sheepish look while the others come over and join us. Zoe greets each the same way, then turns to me. This is the moment, and my anxiety shoots through the roof. I glance at them and then look down, afraid they'll recognize me.

"This is my cousin, Beáta. Beáta, this is Krisztina, Maria, and Balázs."

I extend my hand to each of them, never looking anyone in the eye. They all mumble a greeting and turn back to Zoe. Zoe chats with them about class, and they promise to help her get caught up. After a few minutes, they walk away, leaving us alone again.

Zoe looks at me, a knowing smile on her face. "I told you. They've been in class with you almost every day for months and didn't think twice. You look totally different."

I smile as the relief washes over me.

"The real test will be when you go to school tomorrow."

"Are you crazy? I can't go to school."

"Why not? They didn't even recognize you."

"Hello? Beáta isn't enrolled in the university. Renata is."

"So what? You'll get kicked out of the school if you don't go."

That's the concern that's been on my mind since I came to Zoe and asked her to hide me.

"I need your help." I shake my head. "I mean, I need your help with one more thing."

"What?"

"I need you to talk to my instructors. Tell them I have mononucleosis. Tell them I can't come to class because I'm contagious and that I don't want to flunk out. Get them to give me work I can do from home."

Chapter Eight

Director Toth

Past

After finding Mother bleeding in the bathtub, I ran to the neighbors and asked for help. The neighbor called someone, and men in uniforms came. They put me in the back of a car, and I sat watching them. When the car stopped, the man beside me told me I would be meeting my new family. It turned out to be the best thing that could happen. The house was average size, similar to the one I used to live in. My old house was in south Buda, but this house was in a place called Újpest. When I walked in, the whole family stood in the entry to greet me: the father, mother, and two kids. The father stood at the end, frowning. He talked to the men who brought me. The mother smiled and introduced the children. The kids were named László and Ágota. Ágota, the girl, was older, maybe twelve. László, the boy, was my age.

After talking to the father, the men in the uniforms left, and I was alone with these strange people I had never seen before. They walked me down the hall and showed me the room I would share with László, the boy. In the blink of an eye, my life had changed, and everything was new. I withdrew within myself, avoiding everyone but László.

For the first two weeks, the father never spoke to me, which was preferable. His scowl did nothing but heighten my already high anxiety. One day, as we sat at dinner, he talked to me for the first time. "József, are you happy here?"

I looked up from my stew, surprised he knew my name. "Yes," I said and looked back down. He grunted but said nothing else. I didn't know it at the time, but something had changed. He was accepting me as part of the family. It took time, but eventually, I began to call them Mom and Dad. They treated me like I was their own. It was like I had been born into the family.

When I turned eighteen, I began my military obligation. I liked it. I enjoyed the structure and discipline. After the required years, I stayed on and continued to move up the ranks. I was the youngest captain in the army. I participated in putting down the rebellion of Czechoslovakia. I led my men into battle several times over a week, and that's when I was wounded. I took a bullet in the left shoulder. I spent a couple of weeks in the hospital and months in rehabilitation. When I had healed, my father arranged a new position for me. I was offered an opportunity to join Budapest's Ministry of Internal Affairs. Our mission is to protect Hungary from threats inside and outside the country.

Today is my one-month work anniversary. I've been on the job for thirty days. I've been in nothing but training, and finally, I'm out of headquarters and being sent on a mission. I'm anxious to prove myself. My biological father was a trader. He was taken and imprisoned for his crimes against the state. After that night, I never saw him again. My mother, brokenhearted from his deceit, never recovered. He bears the responsibility for her death. Women are weak. He should have known better. None of that would have happened if he had been loyal to the party and the country. He'd be alive now, and so would she. Dissent breeds sorrow.

We pull up outside a house in District IV, my home district. Officers are standing outside. They nod to us and wave us through. As we reach the porch, a man comes out of the house, followed by two more officers. The lead man frowns and slaps away the hands of the men guiding him. The two officers escort him to a waiting car.

My partner, Agent Juhasz, taps me on the shoulder and motions for me to follow him into the house. Two more officers are inside, along with multiple women in nightgowns and negligees. Two women sit on a couch in the front room. One cries, babbling incoherently. The other consoles her. Both look young. Two other women stand on the staircase, glaring at us as they smoke cigarettes. An older, heavier woman stands talking with the two officers. Juhasz approaches the two officers and says something to one. The man turns and looks at him, nods, then turns back to the woman. Juhasz motions to me, and we climb the stairs, passing the smoking women. They stare at us defiantly as we go by.

When we reach the top of the stairs, Juhasz opens one of the bedroom doors and enters. I follow him but stop short in the doorframe. A woman lays on the bed. She's young, just like the women on the couch downstairs, but unlike them, she's unmoving. Her skin is gray and lifeless. Juhasz approaches and checks her pulse. He looks at me and shakes his head. He scans the room, and I'm unsure what he wants. A wallet sits on a chair next to the bed. He picks it up, opens it, looks around the room one more time, and walks toward me. He exits and walks down the stairs with me following. The officers are still talking to the plump older woman, but the conversation stops as we pass. Juhasz nods to them, and we walk out of the house. As we approach our car, I notice the two officers who had escorted the man out, stand waiting.

"Thanks, men. We'll take it from here," Juhasz instructs.

They nod and walk away.

Juhasz turns to me. "You drive." He hands me the keys, and I slide in behind the wheel while he climbs in the back seat with the man. When we're settled, Juhasz says, "Józef, drive back to headquarters." I put the car in drive and listen to their interaction, occasionally glancing in the rearview mirror.

"What happened?" Juhasz asks.

I look at the man more closely. Should I know him? Why does Juhasz?

"She choked."

"How?"

"I like it rough. She said she did too. It was an accident. I didn't mean to kill her."

"Do you know her? Seen her before?"

"No. She's just the girl I picked out tonight."

"Who knows you were there?"

"Just the people you saw. Nobody else. I didn't tell anyone."

The car goes silent as I drive through the city. When we arrive back at headquarters, Juhasz tells me to wait. He escorts the man into the building and comes back five minutes later. He gets in on the passenger side.

"We have to go back to the house."

I nod and put the car in gear. Once we're back on the road, he starts talking.

"Józef, do you know why you were picked for this?"

I look at him and nod. He pats me on the shoulder.

"Ah, you're a good kid. You'll go far here. Sometimes, we're asked to do things that might seem strange. Our job is to act. Not to question. We have to trust they're for the good of the party. For the good of the country. Understood?"

"I understand, Comrade."

"Good. It's important that what happened tonight never gets out. That man is an important person. He can't be implicated in this. It's our job to make sure he isn't. Understand?"

"Yes, sir."

"We'll go back and do what needs to be done to keep it quiet. You don't mind getting your hands dirty, do you?"

"No, sir."

"Good. You'll go far here, József. Keep your head down, and do what you're told. They'll take care of you."

Chapter Nine

Director Toth

Present

It's an unseasonably warm day, and I decide to walk rather than drive. It's only ten minutes to my destination, and it'll give me a chance to think. I feel rejuvenated as I make my way along Bajcsy Zsilinszky Út. I look to my left and see the Westend Mall. My eyes narrow in disgust. I hate seeing it with its sizeable Western department stores and food court. Options like Burger King and Wendy's. American food. It's changing our country. The Western influence is everywhere. In clothing, media, music, food. Especially here in Budapest. Before long, we'll all be fat Americans speaking English and showing no respect to elders and those in authority.

I can already see it happening with our young people. It's been ten years since the Russians left, and we're worse for it. The Hungarian people are respectful. It's built into our language. You don't speak to an elder like you do to a colleague. You show respect. You speak to them in the third person rather than the first. The other day, as I reached the cashier at the grocery store, I was disgusted by how I was greeted. The young man, at least thirty years younger than me, asked, "How I was?" not "How he was?" the proper language for an elder. I let him have it. I called for his manager and addressed the lack of respect to both of them. I would never have spoken that way at his age. We need to get our country back.

I reach the river and sit on the prearranged bench outside the Parliament Building. I'm five minutes early, so I cross my legs and survey the river and castle on the Buda side. I'm an important man. I'm the leader of the police force in the country and extremely wealthy, although most of my wealth is hidden. It seems issues and problems are ever present. Often, they can be wide in scope and significance. If they were simple, they wouldn't be brought to me. My thoughts return to the biggest of them all. Where's that girl? The one who worked in the internet café. It's just as Gyula had said, she's disappeared. How did she know we'd be coming for her? All I did was sit in the café a few times and send some emails. Who's hiding her?

Out of the corner of my eye, I see the rotund figure of Németh László approaching. When he reaches me, I don't stand. I remain seated, gazing out on the river and Buda Hills.

"How are you today, Mr. Mayor?"

"Good. But not as good as you."

I look at him as he sits beside me. "Oh? Why's that?"

"Because it seems the president is no longer so anxious to replace you."

"Oh?"

He grins and looks out over the river. "Seems he's been impressed with the lack of abductions recently. And he's giving you the credit. He told me the media hadn't asked him about abductions in two weeks. That's the longest it's been in months. You may keep your job after all." He turns back to me and pats me on the shoulder. "I don't know how you did it, but once again, you've made doubters believers."

I smile and turn back to the river. We sit in silence, basking in the sunshine and the good news. The flowing water below us makes me think of Béla. My move to kill him may have seemed rash at the time. Now, the wisdom of it is evident. By killing him, I've eliminated the focus on missing girls. He's no longer asking questions and writing articles, and other news outlets are focused on finding him. A male. Two birds, one stone.

"Oh, I forgot to tell you. I learned who the president had selected to be your successor."

"It went that far?"

"Well, I should say, who he had in mind."

"Who?"

"Rákosi Gyula."

I whip my gaze from the river back to him. "What? How can that be? He works for me. He's not a member of Madl's party."

"I know. I thought that was strange too. But it doesn't matter. As long as the abductions remain low, your job is safe."

My mind drifts back to the girl from the internet café. She's another missing girl, and Gyula is looking for her. I didn't take her, yet she could be the linchpin in all this. Wouldn't that be ironic? A missing girl brings me down. One I didn't even abduct. Suddenly, my anxiousness to find her ratchets up another level.

Chapter Ten

Zsuzsa

I step off the bus, look around to get my bearings, then walk toward my destination. It's later than I hoped, and shadows extend from the mass of ten-story cement apartment buildings surrounding me. I got caught up in the restaurant and didn't leave on time. As usual, Kata wanted to know about Gabor. I almost get the feeling she's living through me. It's not surprising. I'm sure she's lonely. I probably shouldn't say what I say to my boss, but that's me; she knows it by now. I came straight out and asked if she wanted to date again. She acted like she hadn't considered it, but I know it's a deception. Of course, she's thought about it, and she's hesitant. Anyone would be after learning their husband was a trafficker and murderer—the poor woman. I feel for her and told her so.

That's when she opened up. She admitted she's lonely and wants a man, but she doesn't know if she could ever trust one again. I laughed and told her she wasn't alone in feeling that way. I told her she was too trusting before. That she wouldn't do that again, and that's when she confided her biggest fear. Andras had been trafficking for years, and had she not hired Peter, she never would have known. Her husband had lied to her almost every day, and she never knew it. That's when I reminded her that hiring Peter showed she knew something wasn't right. It's the first time since all that happened that I've seen her get emotional. How could I leave? She's been there for me. I had to be there for her.

A man approaches, and I move to the other side of the walk, hoping he goes past. He's a grungy-looking guy, maybe homeless. He steps back in my path.

"Hey, pretty lady, spare some change?"

He moves too close, and I can smell the alcohol on his breath. His palm is turned up. I reach into my jacket, pull out some change, and put it in his hand.

"Thank you. Why don't you come with me? We can share a drink."

He grins, exposing a row of yellow, tangled teeth. Several are missing.

"No, thank you," I say and push past him.

"Hey, what's the hurry? Come back here."

"Leave the lady alone," a voice says. Gabor is on the path before me, glaring at the man.

The man looks at him and raises his hands. "Okay, okay. I'm not trying to start something. Just an invite."

I move closer to Gabor, confused by his presence but grateful.

"Are you okay?" he asks, putting an arm around me.

"I'm fine."

We start walking away from the man in the direction I was already going.

"What are you doing here?"

He shrugs. "I knew you couldn't leave this alone. I had to be sure you'd be safe."

"I can take care of myself."

"I'm not saying you can't. I just don't think it's a good idea you do this on your own."

I look up into his eyes, trying to read them. I can't see anything but honest concern, and it makes me smile. He's really very sweet.

We reach the front of the building and stop.

"You can't come in with me. She'll never talk to me if you're there. Why don't you stay here? I won't be long."

He looks up at the building and then back to me. "Can't I at least come inside?"

I laugh. "Okay. But she can't see you. I have to be alone."

He grabs me by the arm and pulls me to him. He kisses me, and I enjoy the feel of his body against mine.

"Zsuzsa, leave this alone. Don't put her or yourself in more danger. The woman has been through enough. Let it go. Keep yourself safe."

I look into his eyes and try to read his thoughts. Why is he so worried? Is it really just about me? I step away from him. "I just want to talk to her. Five minutes."

A woman exits the building, and I catch the door before it closes. Gabor follows me in, and I turn back to him. "I'll be back soon. Wait here."

He sighs and agrees, and I take the stairs rather than the elevator. When I reach her floor, I'm breathing harder and regretting my decision to take the stairs. I stand and catch my breath and think. What am I going to say to her? I tried to get her to talk last time, and she almost did. Then she noticed her daughter listening, and told me to leave. What can I do to make it different this time? I step up to the door and knock. Nothing. I strike again and still hear nothing. I'm about to turn away when the door opens a crack.

"I thought I told you not to come back."

"You did."

"Then what are you doing here?"

I say the only thing I can think to say: the truth. "I don't know."

She pauses, then opens the door wider. She looks better than last time. Not so drawn. Her eyes are clear. "I can't tell you anything. I can't risk it." She almost yells it as if I'm standing down the stairs instead of in front of her. She steps closer and whispers, "I'm only going to say this once. Look into my family. That's where you'll find the answer." She turns back to her apartment and yells, "I've told you before. Don't ever come back." She slams the door in my face, and I wonder what happened. Did she say what I think she said? What does that mean? Her family? Like genealogy? Eventually, I turn around and head back down the stairs. When I reach the bottom level, Gabor is leaning against the wall.

He sees me, smiles, and comes over. We head for the exit, and he asks, "How'd it go?"

"It didn't. She was home, but she wouldn't talk to me. She slammed the door in my face. I think you're right; I just need to let this go."

We're outside now, and he puts his arm around me and smiles. "You tried. Don't be hard on yourself. It's for the best."

I look up at him, analyze his face, then look back at the path before us.

"Can I give you a ride home? Maybe we can stop and get a bite to eat first?"

I nod, and he smiles and wraps me tighter. As we walk, I can't stop thinking about what she said. What does she mean by "her family," and how will I find out?

Chapter Eleven

Detective Szabo

I step into the small conference room, and relief washes over me. I'm late, but it seems it doesn't matter. All the seats around the table are occupied, except one—Director Toth's chair. The other team members cut their conversation as I walk to the head of the table. Rather than stand, my custom, I sit in the chair and look at each of them.

"Sorry, I'm late. How's everyone?"

They all murmur responses.

"Who wants to start?"

Weekly, we meet and discuss any new developments on missing girls. Although we all share information and work together, each task-force member is assigned primary responsibility for each abduction.

"I'll start," Varga says.

She has a stack of files in front of her, and rather than open each one, she has a summary sheet she refers to. She talks about interviews and new background information on the victims. When it comes time to discuss her new cases, she shrugs and says she has none.

Katona goes next. He doesn't have a summary sheet and has to open each file to jog his memory. His portion takes longer with all the shuffling of files. Still, eventually, he finishes and says he has no new cases either.

Farkas goes last. As usual, he doesn't refer to his summary sheet or open a file. He can look at the name and quote every detail of the case. His memory is impeccable. Maybe that's because each abduction is more personal to him. When he finishes, he also says he has no new cases.

I hadn't realized it, but no new cases were brought to me this week. This has never happened in the time since the task force was created.

"Odd, isn't it?" I muse.

"What do you mean?" Varga asks.

"No new cases all week. Where have the traffickers gone? What's changed?"

Nobody has an answer, and we all sit looking at each other.

Finally, Katona breaks the silence. "Maybe we spooked them in Slovenia. When the bomb went off, we found Officer Kocsis's body and…" His voice trails off when he sees the look I give him.

"Maybe they moved operations. Maybe they aren't in Budapest anymore. They've been in Croatia, Ukraine, and Slovenia. Maybe they're operating in those countries and left Hungary," Varga says.

"I guess that's possible. But why? It's not like we've caught them," I say.

Again, everyone falls silent.

"All right, well, Varga, find out if your theory is true. See if our neighbors are experiencing an uptick in abductions. Let me know when you know. All of you, keep following up on the cases you have. See what we can learn."

I dismiss them and remain at the table. I lean back and rest my hands on my head, lost in thought. How am I going to figure out who the mole is? I'm at a loss on where to go from here. I think it's Farkas, but how can I prove it? I lean forward and brace my hands on the table, preparing to stand, when a thought hits me like a thunderbolt. Weeks ago, in this conference room, Peter had told me Kovacs was waiting for the toxicology report on Agoston, the club manager. He said Kovacs was sure something in it would reveal who the mole was. With Kovacs dying and Peter being arrested, I never followed up on that.

I stand from the table, exit the room, and head down the stairs to the morgue. The temperature is noticeably cooler as I enter the office and see Nemzeti Árpád sitting behind the desk. I have no illusions that my body is some sculpted hulk of granite. But this guy is softer than a marshmallow. He's got a bag of potato chips, a pastry, and a large soda on his desk. He looks at me, frowns, then goes back to analyzing whatever is on his computer. I walk up and stand next to his desk.

"Árpád?"

He grunts and doesn't look at me.

"Do you have a minute?"

He still doesn't look at me, and I get the feeling he didn't even hear me. I pick up the bag of potato chips, take out a few, and cram them in my mouth. That does it. He glares at me and yanks the bag from my hand.

"What can I do for you, Detective?"

"Do you remember that club manager who died a few weeks back? The one Detective Kovacs was investigating?"

"The one that was poisoned?"

"Yeah."

"Of course. That was the first time I've seen someone die of arsenic poisoning. That was fascinating." He takes a bite of his pastry, and some of the jelly plops on his shirt. From the looks of it, it's not the only thing he's eaten today.

"I bet his mother doesn't describe it as fascinating."

We glare at each other.

"I heard Kovacs had the report delivered to his office. What happened to it?"

"You heard wrong. Kovacs came down here and got it himself. He put it in an envelope and had me write his name on it, then he left."

"Really? What happened to the envelope?"

"Someone must have recognized my handwriting and brought it back to me. It sat on my desk for about a week."

"Where is it now?"

"Detective Farkas came and asked me about it. I gave it to him."

I can't mask the surprise.

"Is there a problem?"

"No. I just didn't know he had it. I'll go ask him about it. Thanks."

I exit the room and head back up the stairs. Farkas came and asked for the envelope? How did he know? Then I remember. After Peter had told me about the envelope, I told Varga and Farkas about it. We all wondered what was inside. It's not surprising that Farkas would come and ask for it. But why didn't he tell me he had it? Something isn't right. I think I know who our mole is. I just need to figure out how to draw him out.

Chapter Twelve

Peter

Peter takes the menu from the hostess as he sits at a table by himself at the Dubarry in Pest. The restaurant lies on the Pest side of the river between the Chain and Elizabeth bridges. It's his first time being here, and he hadn't planned on coming. Since returning to Budapest, he's been on a mission to learn who Director Toth might be working with. Several times, he's followed Németh László, the Újpest mayor, with little result. From all outward appearances, the mayor seems to be nothing more than that. Not once has he met the director with Peter watching. Peter decided to change things up and follow Toth's wife. He's unsure what he'll learn but wants to know how much the woman knows.

Unfortunately, the hostess has seated him far away from his target. Peter had warily followed after her, concerned that she could be meeting the director. Being spotted by him would be about the worst thing for Peter, who now sits with several tables between him and Mrs. Toth. Mrs. Toth joined a table with two other women she was obviously friendly with. They haven't stopped talking since she arrived. After a few minutes, the server comes by and greets Peter. He points to a table next to the women and asks if he can move over there because of its proximity to the windows and the view of the river.

"Of course," the young woman replies and ushers him to the table. She tells him she'll give him a few more minutes to review the menu and then return. Peter thanks her and looks at the course options while listening closely to the table beside him. Mrs. Toth is doing the talking.

"It's just hard being a politician's wife. I never thought I'd say that. I always thought I'd be a police officer's wife. To tell you the truth, I've never paid attention to politics. But now it seems like our lives are dependent on it. I try to stay informed. Especially with what's going on with József now."

All three women look about the same age, and Peter wonders if they were friends when they were kids.

"What do you mean? What's going on with József?" the pretty blonde with short hair says. The woman has striking blue eyes and long eyelashes.

Mrs. Toth looks around, leans forward, and drops her voice. "The president has been angling to replace him as director of the National Police."

Both women's eyes go wide with surprise. Mrs. Toth nods.

"József said it's all due to politics too. He said the president wants him removed because they belong to different political parties."

"He can't do that, can he?" the brunette with wisps of gray in her hair says.

"I guess he can. I've never seen József so worried."

The ladies' server returns and they all place their orders. After they're done, the blonde asks, "What would József do if he wasn't director?"

"I don't know. He's been in the police since he was out of the army, over thirty years. To tell you the truth, and don't say this to anyone, but I kind of wish it would happen."

"What?" both women exclaim. They look at each other, and the brunette leans forward, whispering, "What do you mean? You want him to lose his job?"

"I kind of do. Is that terrible?"

"Why?" asks the blonde.

"Because, ever since our son was killed, he's been different. I don't think he's been able to deal with that loss. He blames himself. I told him it wasn't his fault. Máté was a grown man and wanted to become a cop. I can tell József doesn't hear me. It's like a part of him died with Máté."

Peter's server comes back and asks for his order. He tries to listen to the conversation and order simultaneously but only gets bits and pieces. The other women asked if they would be okay financially if Toth lost his job, and his wife admitted that she didn't know but thought so.

The conversation turns to a lighter subject as they discuss vacation plans. Peter takes a sip of his sparkling water and looks around. His gaze stops on a beautiful woman sitting on the other side of the restaurant. She's staring at him, and his eyes lock on the familiar face. Peter feels his heart rate quicken as she stands and moves toward him. Unsure what to do, he stands and motions with his head for her to follow him. He finds a hallway and walks down it toward the bathrooms. He turns and sees the woman is still following him and has almost reached him. He anxiously waits, wondering what her reaction will be.

"Peter? Wha...what are you doing here?"

"Hi, Kata."

She has surprise and uncertainty in her eyes. "I thought you were...gone?"

"I was. I just got back a few days ago."

She frowns at him, and he wonders if she doubts his story. It's clear she has a thousand questions but isn't sure where to start.

"I'm sorry I haven't come to see you. I couldn't. I hope you understand."

"Why? What's going on? How are you back?"

Peter quickly explains how he went to jail and was released. He describes how he was threatened never to return to Hungary but couldn't let go of the trafficking. He tells her he had to sneak back into the country to save someone. He's been keeping a low profile as he works to uncover the truth. As he explains, he can see her relax. The doubt in her eyes gives way to concern. "Anyway, I've had to be really careful. I knew the traffickers were likely watching you, Zsuzsa, and Szép Ilona's. I couldn't contact you and risk being seen."

Kata nods. "Do you know who's doing the trafficking?"

"I do. I just have to figure out how to prove it, which is even harder than it might sound."

"Why?"

Peter hesitates and then peers at her closely. "Did Andras ever mention knowing a man named Toth József?"

Kata shakes her head. "Is that the trafficker?"

"Yes."

"Why is it so hard to prove?"

"It's probably better if I don't tell you that. Forget I mentioned that name."

Kata gives him a look but doesn't push it.

"How are you? How's Zsuzsa?"

"I'm okay. The restaurant is doing better. I think I might be able to keep it going and make some money."

"That's great. I'm so happy for you."

She nods and smiles. "Zsuzsa's good. She was pretty upset when I gave her your letter."

"I know. I wanted to tell her I got out. I just couldn't."

"I know. But it hit her pretty hard. I've never seen her like that. There's something I need to tell you."

Peter eyes her, waiting.

"She's started dating someone else."

Peter nods, but Kata sees the absence of surprise in his eyes. "You knew."

He nods.

"How?"

"I wanted to see her. I sat outside her apartment one night and saw her with him."

She steps closer and rubs his arm, looking into his eyes. "She likes him. He really is a beautiful man. But I wouldn't give up hope. I know how much she cares for you. She still thinks about you all the time."

Peter feels some hope for the first time in days. "Tell me about him. Who is he? How did they meet?"

"His name is Gabor. They grew up together in the same neighborhood. He's in advertising. He's had some great ideas to help us at the restaurant. He's divorced and has a child. One day, he just showed up at the restaurant. It was totally random. They hadn't seen each other for years and years. He's pursued her pretty hard. He comes in a lot. Like I said, he's strikingly handsome. I think she was flattered by his interest. She had a crush on him when they were young." Kata, seeing the look on his face, reaches back out and rubs his shoulder again. "Peter, I know you care about her. But can I give you some advice? You can't wait any longer or you'll lose her forever. Zsuzsa's taken with Gabor, and the longer you remain out of her life, the more likely you'll never be able to get back in. If you want her, you've got to show her."

Chapter Thirteen

Director Toth

Past

It's been five years since I started at the Ministry of Internal Affairs. The time has been good to me. I've married, and we have a son. I've also been promoted once and expect to be again today. Yesterday, we learned our captain is moving positions. They'll select a new captain, and everyone thinks it will be me. At first, I didn't believe it, but now I do. I've got an excellent record. I've trained multiple new officers and am the youngest senior agent on the force. People say I'm on the fast track to leadership. Today might be the first significant step.

The deputy director has called a special meeting to announce the change. I arrive a couple minutes before the session is due to start, and most of the seats are already filled. I see Juhasz and a few of my buddies. They wave me over, and I sit down. Several pat me on the back, and when I look at them, they flash me a knowing smile. After a few minutes, the deputy director walks to the podium.

"As you know, our charge is to protect and serve Hungary. Our leaders rely on us to root out dissension, to keep the peace, and to protect the country from anarchy. Captain Barna has been a wonderful example to all of you. But, like most things in life, it's time for change. Barna deserves a new challenge. I've called you here today to announce the new captain."

Juhasz elbows me in the ribs. A few other guys look at me and nod.

"I'm pleased to announce your new captain will be Matos Norbert."

Silence.

Eyes flash to Norbert, then back to me.

"Captain Matos, why don't you come forward and say a few things to your new men."

As Norbert makes his way to the podium, Juhasz puts an arm around me, and several guys give me an empathetic look. I keep my eyes on Norbert as he walks to the front. He's average height with a thin build. He wears a pair of glasses and has curly, brown hair. I've known him for a couple years. He's barely been around for longer than that. He's probably the newest senior agent. In all the speculation leading up to today's announcement, I never heard anyone guess it would be him.

He thanks the deputy director, pledges his loyalty to the party and the country, and tells us all he looks forward to working with us. We cheer, and the deputy director releases us.

After the meeting, I walk to my desk and busy myself with work. I'm only there a few minutes when ex-Captain Barna comes by. "Toth, step into my office for a minute." I stand and follow him. He closes the door and motions to me. "Take a seat." He moves around his desk and stares at me after sitting down. "I understand many men were speculating that you'd be the next captain."

I shrug, unsure what to say to this.

"Norbert's a good man, but it should have been you." He must see the surprise in my eyes because he asks, "Why do you think it wasn't?"

I frown. I've been asking myself the same question and haven't come up with an answer.

"You haven't earned the trust of your superiors."

"What? Why not?"

He leans back in his chair and puts his feet up. "Oh, sure, your comrades love you. But even they don't know if they can trust you."

I'm shocked. I want to lash out and tell him he's wrong. Instead, I say, "Sir, I've done everything asked of me. Isn't my record clear on that?"

"Oh, I'm not talking about your record. Nobody works harder than you do, József. I'm talking about after work. I'm talking about going out with the boys. You go home to your wife and son. You put off an air of judgment. Like you judge your comrades for their behavior. Nobody wants that. If you want to move up, you have to be all in. Not just at work."

I leave his office, sit at my desk, and think about what he said. I thought I'd earn their respect by going home and not going out with the boys. That nothing could be used against me. I never would have imagined that it would work the other way. That others would question my loyalty.

"Hey, sorry about that, Toth."

I look up and see Juhasz standing over me. I shrug. "It's okay. I wasn't expecting to be captain. You guys were wrong, not me."

He nods and starts to walk away.

"Hey, anybody going out tonight?" I call after him.

He looks at me with surprise. "Probably. Why?"

"Maybe I can tag along."

"You? Okay. Great. Let's do it. I'll let the guys know."

I smile, and he walks away. I've heard stories about what "going out" means to these men, and I wonder how much is embellished. I guess I'll find out.

Chapter Fourteen

Director Toth

Present

I sit at my desk and stare at the clock. He's late again. Rákosi Gyula has worked for me for years, and I could have counted the times he'd been late on two fingers. That number has doubled this week. What's going on? Is it intentional? Is this related to him being the president's choice to replace me? Has he lost respect? No longer values my position over him?

A knock at the door. I call for him to enter. He walks in carrying a notepad and pen. We stare at each other as he approaches the desk and sits opposite me.

"You're late."

"I lost track of time. This case continues to get more interesting."

I planned to unload on him, but this revelation intrigues me. "How so?"

"Some new evidence has come up. Two pieces, actually."

I've been expecting this. But I anticipated only one.

"What new evidence?"

"We got a tip on where the body was."

I do my best to act surprised. "Oh?"

"Yeah, turns out our boy Béla wasn't as squeaky clean as we thought. Or at least someone wants us to think that. He might have had a girlfriend. Or at least a woman he was seeing. Nobody knows the girl, other than how she made her money."

"She was a hooker?"

"Yep." Gyula leans back and puts his foot on the opposite knee.

"Okay, so he goes and sees a hooker. But how did he die?"

"Well, that's where it gets kind of hazy."

"How so?"

"We aren't sure if he drowned or was electrocuted."

"Come again?"

"He was found in a bathtub. A blow-dryer in the water next to him."

"Hmm." I lean back in my chair and steeple my hands, resting my elbows on the arms. "Where was the girl?"

"In the living room. We found her first. A gunshot wound to the head. It was made to look like a murder-suicide."

"But you don't think it was?"

"Nope."

"Why not?"

"The whole thing was staged."

"How did you come to that conclusion?"

He slides a couple of photos onto my desk. I pick up the first one; it's of the girl.

"Look at the way she's laying. The gunshot wound is on the left side of her head. You can't see it from this angle, but the bullet exited on the other side. We searched the room—no sign of it and no casing either. Then there's the lack of blood on the floor. She wasn't shot there; she was planted."

"Why would someone plant her there?"

He shrugs.

"Any leads on who might have done it?"

"No, and I don't think we'll get any either."

"Why do you say that?"

"Because whoever did this knew we'd know the body was planted, but they didn't care. It was more important not to have shell casings and bullets to analyze. They planted the bodies, knew we'd know they were planted, but gave us nothing to work with. Same thing with Béla."

"So where were they killed?"

"We don't know. My guess is Béla was killed on the riverbank where we originally searched. The girl, I'm not sure. I doubt they were killed together. Maybe they didn't even know each other."

"That's just speculation on your part."

"True."

I bite my cheek and look out the window. "Anything else?"

"No, we'll keep investigating, but I'm not hopeful."

"We're going to have to notify the press."

He nods and stands. "I have one request."

"What's that?"

"Don't notify them until I talk to the widow. I don't want her to hear he was with a hooker when we aren't sure he was. I'd rather he keep some dignity."

I nod and tell him he has until the end of the day. He turns to leave. It's a reasonable request, but I won't honor it. He likely knew he was Madl's choice to replace me and never told me. Also, I never liked Béla anyway. I killed him. But he had it coming. He had a chance to live and take a handsome payout. It's his own fault he's dead.

Gyula's almost reached the door when a thought pops into my head. "Hey, you said two pieces of evidence. What was the other?"

He looks at me quizzically.

"When you came in, you said there were two new pieces of evidence. You found Béla's body. What was the other? I assume you weren't referring to the girl."

He nods. "Béla was talking to someone else about the missing girls."

That revelation hits me like a thunderbolt, but I remain calm. "What? Who?"

"A reporter with Duna Television. They were exchanging emails. I'm not sure they ever met, but they certainly talked on the phone."

I sit looking at him. Several questions run through my mind.

"Anyway, we went to talk to her. He told her about his meeting with the 'Concerned Citizen' that night."

My eyes narrow as I look at him.

"But she's missing too. She hasn't been seen since being fired for interviewing a girl about trafficking on air. We're looking for her now."

That's news to me too. I didn't know the girl was fired.

"Okay, let me know when you find her."

He shuts the door, and I stand and walk to the window. I cross my arms and look out at the city below. My jaw clenches and unclenches. We should have waited. One more day could have made all the difference. Gyula would have known about Lili. We could have planted evidence about them running away together. Being in a relationship. That would have been perfect. A thought pops in my head and I slap the window with my hand. Gyula's had access to Béla's email for a week. He's known about Lili for longer than a day. He knew about her before they found Béla's body. He's been holding back information from me. I grit my teeth. What else is he hiding? And why tell me this now?

I walk over and pick up the phone. I dial the number and wait for an answer.

"Hi, Boss."

"Where's Lili, the reporter?"

"We don't know. Our guy was going to pick her up when someone else grabbed her first. They drove out of town, and he lost their trail in Budakeszi. She hasn't surfaced."

"What about the girl from the internet café?"

A hesitation on the other end of the line.

"We can't find her either."

"Don't you find it ironic that we abduct girls, yet we can't find these ones?" I snap. "Why are you failing me?"

Silence on the other end of the phone, and a thought hits me. Gyula has them. He's been ahead of me since he started investigating Béla. He knows, and he's holding these girls while he builds a case against me. "He knows."

"Who knows? Knows what?"

"Rákosi Gyula. He's the one who took these girls. Lili was emailing Béla, and he knew we'd be coming for her. He knew we'd be after the internet-café girl. He's behind it. He's the only possible answer."

We both consider the implications.

"What do you want me to do?"

"Find the girls! I don't care what it takes. Find them." I take a deep breath, collect myself, and lower my voice. "He hasn't exposed us because he doesn't have enough evidence yet. We still have time, but we can't wait around until he does."

"Yes, sir. Can I make a suggestion?"

I say nothing.

"I think we should follow him. Maybe he'll lead us to the girls."

There's an inherent risk to this. He might know he's being followed.

"Put your best person on it. Find them!"

I slam down the phone and look at the pictures on my credenza. I've shut down abductions in the city while we wait for the political heat to blow over. I'm giving up thousands of forints a day. Now, Gyula and these girls could be my undoing. I can't sit around and wait. He could be ready to expose me anytime. I've got to act. I pick up my phone and call my secretary.

"How can I help you, sir?"

"Do you have a pen handy? I want you to draft a press release. Béla, the reporter, has been found."

"That's wonderful!"

"He's dead."

Silence on the other end.

"I want the press notified immediately."

Chapter Fifteen

Zsuzsa

I lock the office door, walk down the hall, and enter the restaurant's main dining area. My heart drops as I look at the bar and see Zoltan sitting there. He's the only customer left. I really don't want to deal with this today. I walk toward him, and just as I'm about to say something, Csaba, our bartender, stands from below the bar. I exhale, feeling a great sense of relief. We lock eyes, and I motion with my head toward Zoltan. Csaba gives me a nod and turns to him.

"Zoltan, I'm not going to tell you again. Time to go home."

Zoltan looks at Csaba, splashes one last swig down his throat, and slams the tumbler down on the bar. It thuds against the polished wood. I don't think he meant it. He's so inebriated he doesn't have full control of his movements. He swings his leg off the stool and stands on wobbly knees. He looks over at me with glassy eyes. "Zsuzsa, will you help me to the door?"

"Not a chance," I say and glare at him. The last time, he groped me before exiting.

He shrugs and waddles to the exit. I follow him, making sure not to get too close. When he reaches the door, he turns and says, "I'm sorry, Zsuzsa. You're just too beautiful. I couldn't help myself."

Something snaps inside me. I've had enough of men claiming they can't help leering or rubbing up against me. Excusing their behavior by saying "you're too beautiful" or "so damn sexy." When I was younger, I might have put up with it. Not anymore.

"That's not an excuse to disrespect me. Do you think I want to be treated like that?"

His eyes drop, and he looks at the floor. "No, I'm sorry." He pushes the door open and exits the restaurant. I lock the door behind him and go back to Csaba.

"What was that all about?" he asks.

"A couple weeks ago, I helped him to the door, and he groped me on his way out. He thought it was funny. I didn't."

Csaba shakes his head and looks around. "I think we're all set here. You ready to go?"

"Yep."

I grab my coat, and he cuts the lights. We exit through the kitchen door and part ways. He lives north of the restaurant, and I'm south. He crosses the street while I turn and head for the bus stop. With a start, I see the bus is early. It's already sitting at the station. I pick up my pace; I'm only about four hundred feet away. When I reach a hundred feet, the door closes, and the bus pulls away. I call after it and start running, but it's gone before I can reach it. I look down at my watch. It's ten now. After ten, the buses run less frequently. If I wait for the next one, I'll stay at least a half hour. That's silly for a ten-minute walk home. Yes, I'm exhausted from a long day, but the memory of my last walk makes me hesitate. What if Gabor hadn't been there? What plans did that stranger have for me?

I look behind me. The streets are empty, other than an occasional car. I decide to walk, but I choose to take the long way. It'll keep me on busier streets. Last time, my tail waited until I was in a neighborhood. As I walk, I frequently look back, ensuring I'm alone. Is this my new normal? Am I always going to feel nervous and afraid to be alone? Will I ever feel safe again?

Maybe. I guess I have two choices. I could extract myself from all of this. Pretend the trafficking isn't happening. Forget I was ever abducted myself. In that case, they might leave me alone. Nothing's happened since the night I was followed. Could I ever really do that, though? I watched as young girls worked in the restaurant and disappeared. I didn't know what was happening, but I knew Andras wasn't good. I still dream about some of those girls. I wonder where they went.

Plus, I've got new information now. The mother in Újpest told me to investigate her family. I plan to, but I'm not sure how. Should I contact Szabo? Can I trust him? Maybe Gabor's right. Perhaps if I do nothing, they'll leave her and me alone. What can I do about the trafficking? I'm not the police.

I near my apartment building and look back. Is that what I think it is? I peer more closely. I think I see the dark shadow of a man walking toward me. Fear grips me, and I start to run. I can see my building ahead. I accelerate and reach the stairs before daring to look again. Nobody's there. Did I imagine the whole thing? Oh, I'm so sick of this. I open the front door and walk into the building. My chest rises and falls from the run and adrenaline kick.

I go up the elevator and enter my apartment. I flip on the kitchen light, put my purse on the table, and hang up my coat. I'm so exhausted. I just want to crash. Curl up in my warm bed and put my fears aside for another day. But I know I shouldn't. I'll regret it in the morning.

I walk into my bedroom and angle toward the bathroom when a powerful arm grabs me. A hand clamps over my mouth, and panic surges. They've got me again. I start to fight when a familiar voice says, "Zsuzsa, it's me, Peter." I hear the words, but I can't fathom them. I keep fighting, but he holds his hand over my mouth. He's much stronger than I am. I feel his breath on my ear. He's so close. "It's me. I didn't mean to scare you, but I need to talk to you."

It is Peter. I stop fighting, and he releases me. I turn and look up at him. A surge of emotion courses through me as I stare into his eyes. He smiles that familiar grin, and I smile back, my chest rising and falling as I gain control. I never thought I'd see him again. How is he standing here in my bedroom?

"Peter? You're back?"

"I'm back."

"How?"

He shrugs and raises an eyebrow. "I couldn't stay away."

I can't help myself; I lean forward and throw my arms around him. He holds me until I step back again.

"But how did you get back here?"

"My brother-in-law is with the State Department in the US. He got me back in the country without presenting my passport. Nobody can know I'm here. That's why I had to surprise you like this."

We stand looking at each other, unsure what to say.

Finally, he starts. "I'm sorry I left the way I did."

"Yeah." What else can I say? He broke my heart, leaving and not telling me. Plus, there's the way he acted in the jail. I don't know if I can forgive that.

He steps forward and grabs my hand. "It's good to see you."

I look up at him and force a smile. "It's good to see you too. I'm sorry. I'm just so shocked."

"I know."

"You hurt me with what you said in the jail. I know why you did it, but it still hurt."

"I know. But I had to. I knew someone was listening."

I nod and sit down on the bed. My head is spinning.

"I know who's behind the trafficking. I couldn't tell you in there."

"Who?"

"The head of the National Police. Director Toth József. He, or someone who works for him, was listening to our conversation. I was put in jail to shut me up."

I figured that much. As I watch him, I can't help my conflicted feelings. I'm so happy to see him, to know he's safe and well. But I thought he was gone from my life. I've moved on.

"Look, Peter, I'm happy to see you and that you're back. But I must tell you, I've started dating someone else."

Peter nods. "I know. I saw you the other night."

I feel a flash of irritation. *He's been watching me?*

He must see my anger because he says, "I wanted to see you. I waited outside, hoping to glimpse you, then you came home with him."

I say nothing.

"Look, I'm worried about you. I want to make sure you're safe."

"What do you mean?"

Peter puts his hands in his jacket and shrugs. "How well do you know this guy you've been dating? How did you meet? Where did he come from?"

I feel a flash of irritation. What business is this of his? Did he forget he left? I sat around here crying for him, trying to devise a plan to get him out of jail, and he was back in America sipping drinks with his family, enjoying a vacation.

"I've known him since we were kids. He came into the restaurant a few weeks ago. I hadn't seen him in years. But we talked, and he asked me out. I enjoy being with him."

"Okay. Maybe he's a great guy. I'd be lying if I said I'm not jealous. Maybe I'm not being fair to him. But don't you think it's a little strange that this guy shows back up in your life after so long? And just after I've disappeared? The timing is suspicious, don't you think?"

"Peter, you don't know him. He saved me once. Someone was following me home. He was here and rescued me."

"You're right. I don't know him. I want you to be happy. But just be careful, okay? Make sure you can trust him." He turns to leave, then asks, "Did you ever go see that woman in Újpest? The one whose daughter was taken?"

"Yes. She wouldn't talk to me. She's terrified. She did say that if I wanted to know why, I should investigate her family."

He frowns. "Her family?"

"Yes. I didn't know what she meant. Then she slammed the door. I haven't been able to investigate it."

"Don't. You've been mixed up in this enough. I'll see what I can find out."

He turns to leave again, and I say, "Peter?" When he turns around, I tell him, "It's good to see you. I wish things had turned out differently between us."

He looks at me and starts to say something, but he stops. Finally, he says, "It's good to see you too. I care about you. Be safe."

Chapter Sixteen

Detective Szabo

I sit in my car and wait. I know he's got to be leaving soon. He's a go-getter. He's in the office early and often the last to leave. But this is late, even for him. I look at the clock on my dash: seven thirty p.m. Doesn't he get hungry? I swear, I never see the guy eat. Maybe that's the secret to staying trim. I look down at my gut. Perhaps that's how I could lose this spare tire. I shake my head. No, if it takes that, I want to be fat. Food is one of my only pleasures. Eh, who am I kidding? It's my *only* pleasure. It's been years since I've been with a woman and never with a woman like Zsuzsa. If Zsuzsa is filet mignon, my ex-wife is ground beef with bones.

Oh, Zsuzsa. Do you have any idea what you do to a man like me? I let myself fantasize about her: her long, blond hair, bright eyes, pouty lips, and impressive figure. I can only imagine what it might be like to caress her soft skin. She really is a marvel. If she would even look my way, give me any chance, I'd give up eating. I'd do whatever she wanted. I'd run five miles a day. That gets me thinking: what does she want? Peter. I saw the way she looked when she came out of the jail. What was it about Peter that attracted her? He's not quite as tall as me, but he's still tall. He's older than me. He's got a muscular build but nothing outrageous. Is that it? Is it as simple as he's thinner and in better shape? Is that all I need to do? He was a detective, I'm a detective. Maybe I do have a chance? I look at the can of cola sitting next to me, roll down my window, and empty it onto the street. That's it. I'm going to lose weight. My diet starts tonight.

The door across the street swings open, and Detective Farkas exits the Hungarian National Police Headquarters. It's about time. I shift into first gear and slowly pull out. Farkas walks two blocks to the parking garage where those of us not named Toth have to park. I wait until I see his green Opel pull onto the street, then I start to follow, ensuring a reasonable distance. We head east, eventually ending up on Andrássy Út. He lives close to here. I can't help my feeling of disappointment. It looks like I sat around for nothing. I guess there's one silver lining: I get to eat. I'm hungry. Maybe I'll start the diet tomorrow.

Last night, after everyone left, I got Árpád from IT to log me on to Farkas's computer. I made up some story about him forgetting to give me something. Because I'm now Farkas's boss, Árpád didn't ask any questions. I searched through all of Farkas's files for an hour but found nothing about him being a trafficker. No emails either. After that, I searched through his desk but still came up empty.

Farkas reaches his home street now but doesn't turn. I feel a rush of excitement as I follow. Another couple blocks, and he arrives at Heroes' Square. He parks beside the huge marble plaza. I drive past him as he exits his car, keeping my head down. I circle the square as he walks to the center and sits on one of the steps below the massive statue there. I find a parking spot up the road, exit, and walk back toward the square but don't enter. I notice a large tree across the street from the plaza at the National Museum. I walk over and stand under the tree in the shadows. From this spot, I have a great view of Farkas, but with the cover of the tree, he can't see me.

After about five minutes, he stands as another man approaches. Even from this distance, I can see the man is short. I'd recognize him anywhere. It's Rákosi Gyula. Gyula motions to him, and he sits back down as Gyula joins him on the step. For ten minutes, they sit talking. Finally, Gyula gets up and leaves. Farkas waits another five minutes, then walks to his car. I realize I'm going to lose him if I don't hurry. I break into a jog as I rush back to my vehicle. It's only about five hundred feet away, but I'm breathing like a locomotive when I reach it. As quick as I can, I pull back onto Andrássy Út and search for the green Opel.

My heart sinks as I realize I've lost it. I pull to the side of the road and wait, checking each car that passes. After a few minutes, I give up and drive to Farkas's apartment building. A pang of disappointment strikes as I pass his empty parking space. I circle the block, then park down the street where I can keep my eyes on it. I shut off the car lights and wait.

I process what I just saw. Rákosi Gyula? Why would he be meeting with Farkas? Panic rises in my chest as I realize what this might mean. If Farkas is the mole in the task force, and he's meeting with Gyula, that means Gyula is probably involved also. Maybe Gyula is running the whole thing? My hand goes to my forehead as I look at the steering wheel, considering the implications. If Gyula's involved, then I've made another major mistake. Two days ago, I opened up to Gyula and told him I suspected someone in the task force was a trafficker. My hand drops to my chin as I think back to the conversation. Gyula acted nonchalant about the whole thing. It was almost like he didn't believe it or didn't care. Was that an act? Did I give him the information he was seeking?

I groan and shake my head. "Stupid!" I slam my hand on the steering wheel. Somehow, I've got to make this right. My stomach growls, and my thoughts return to food. I know it's a coping mechanism. Whenever I make a mistake, or life doesn't go my way, I eat. I've been that way for years. I want pizza, and if Farkas isn't here, why should I stay? I turn the ignition and pull out in search of comfort. I'll think more clearly on a full stomach.

Chapter Seventeen

Renata

I sit on a park bench and stare at the Budapest University of Technology and Economics, my school, and try to control my breathing. I know I'm taking a risk. But what choice do I have? I can't do this on my own. I need help.

Math has always been second nature for me. It's felt like a language I've always known. As natural as Hungarian. Agnes was the opposite. We'd sit in class, and the teacher would demonstrate a new algebraic concept that made sense. It felt natural. I'd look at her, and I'd see her eyes had glazed over. I'd know she'd be asking for tutoring help that night. My heart hurts at the thought. Oh, Agnes...I miss you so much. Zoe, my friend from school, has been great. But Agnes had been my best friend since we were five. She was a part of me. It feels like half my soul was stolen. Every night, when I try to sleep, I see her in my mind. She's lying face down on the floor, a pool of blood surrounding her. One lifeless eye staring at me. Then that big, fat guy, her killer, appears on the threshold to the kitchen. I bolt, and he runs after me. He chases me down the stairs but can't catch me.

Where is he now? He claimed to be the police. Are the police involved in the trafficking? I shake my head. That's the problem, I don't know. Every man has been different. First, there was David in the club. He was nothing like that guy. So smooth, so handsome. Then, the guy in Ukraine, the one I escaped from, he was foreign. Now, this colossal man claiming to be a cop. Is he the leader? Are they working for him?

I feel myself hyperventilating and take a few deep breaths. I can't think about that right now. I have to focus on what I'm about to do. I stand and walk to the entrance of the school and enter. Most of my fellow classmates have cleared out now. There's only a scattering of them as I walk down the hallway. One girl does a double-take at me. Is it because of the way I look or because she recognizes me? I reach the classroom of Professor

Takács and peer inside. This is it. Once I go in, there's no turning back. I can see her wiping the blackboard. She's clearing today's lesson, and I wish she wouldn't. I need that.

I step inside, and she sees me from the corner of her eye. She turns to look at me, and her look goes from surprise to wariness. She doesn't know me.

"Hi, Professor."

"Hi…"

She continues to stare, waiting for me to say something. I look around the room, making sure we're alone. I step closer. "You probably don't recognize me. My name's Renata. I'm in your ten o'clock class."

Her eyes narrow, then widen in surprise as recognition dawns. "Renata. I didn't recognize you. Are you okay? I haven't seen you in a while, and you've…changed."

I take another step closer and lower my voice. "I know. Can I confide in you?" I felt comfortable with her immediately. She's the kind of person who exudes kindness. She truly loves her job and cares for her students. I knew that from my first day of class.

"Of course. Let's sit down." She puts a hand on my shoulder and guides me to a desk in the front row. She sits in the one beside me. "Tell me what's going on."

I want to trust her, but I can't. At least, not completely. Plus, who would believe the truth anyway? It sounds fantastic, even in my own mind. I decide to ease into it.

"I haven't been coming to class because of a family problem. I don't want to get into all of it, but I need not to be seen by certain people for a while. That's why I look like this. That's also why I had Zoe bring my work home to me, and she told you I have mononucleosis. I'm sorry that I lied. I hope you understand."

She looks at me, a line creasing her forehead. "Oh, you poor girl. It's okay. You don't need to tell me everything. I understand, and I'm sorry."

"Thank you."

"Are you okay? Are you safe?"

I'm not, but I don't want to get into all that with her. "I'm okay."

She reaches over and rubs my shoulder. "But there's something you should know." She stops and stares into my eyes, seeming to hesitate, or maybe she's searching for the right words. "Your sister was here this morning."

"What?"

"Yes. She said they hadn't heard from you in weeks, and your mother's concerned."

I stare at her. How could my little sister, Anna, have been here? Would she have come all the way from Szerencs? Maybe they heard about Agnes and are looking for me. "Anna?"

"I don't know. She didn't give me her name. She said she's been trying to find you. She was a pretty woman. Looked like you. Or the before you." She smiles as she says it, but it's the "woman" that strikes me like a lightning bolt. Anna is pretty, but nobody would refer to her as a woman. She's only twelve.

"What did you tell her?"

"I didn't tell her much. I told her you've been sick, and a classmate has taken your work home."

"Did you tell her who? Which classmate?"

She taps her finger to her lips. "Hmm...I don't know. Yes, I think I told her it was Zoe."

Panic rises in my chest. "Did she ask anything else?"

"No. I told her I couldn't tell her anything more. She thanked me and left."

I stand from the desk, the homework forgotten. I've got to find Zoe. She's in danger.

Chapter Eighteen

Peter

Peter sits in the white Volkswagen van, watching the house. Last night, after seeing Gabor leave Szép Ilona's, he followed him here. He arrived around nine p.m. and never left. Finally, after waiting for two hours, Peter went and got some sleep. He came back at five a.m. and has been waiting ever since. It's now after eight. If he's lucky, Peter got four hours of sleep, but he's got to know. Since leaving Zsuzsa's apartment, he can't let go of their conversation. Why did Gabor suddenly show up at her restaurant after not seeing her for so long? The timing is too suspicious. No, if he's honest with himself, it's much more than that. Is it crazy to hope the guy is dirty? He doesn't want to endanger Zsuzsa, but jealousy is burning him up. He didn't come back to stop Toth only. He came back for Zsuzsa. How can he walk away after being so close to her a few days ago? Every part of him longs for her. He knows he should investigate the woman's family in Újpest. That's a piece of information he's been dying to get. Only concern for one person could prevent him from following up on that lead.

A movement at the house brings him back to the present. Gabor has exited his front door and is walking toward the gate. Peter groans. Prancing along beside Gabor is a large black Rottweiler with a studded collar as if this wasn't complicated enough. Gabor yells at the dog, and it backs up from the gate as he opens it. He gets in his shiny red BMW, pulls out onto the street, gets out, locks the gate, and heads back to the car. Peter watches all this from the floor of the van. He had brought a mirror with him and angled it to see Gabor's house. The last thing he needs is for Gabor to see him, even if he isn't sure Gabor would know him.

Peter waits five minutes, ensuring the BMW hasn't returned, then exits the van. As he approaches the house, he crosses the street and hears the bellow of Gabor's dog. He nonchalantly throws the final quarter of the breakfast sandwich he's been eating into the yard and continues up the road. He walks around the neighborhood for twenty minutes, giving the medication time to set in.

Peter reaches Gabor's street again and approaches the house. This time, only silence. He walks up to the gate and pokes his head over the fence. Sprawled out along the pebbled driveway is the dog. His back faces Peter, but judging by how ravenous he was earlier when Peter had approached, the medication has taken effect. Peter looks around the neighborhood, makes sure nobody is watching, and climbs the gate. When he's on the other side, he moves to the back of the house and investigates the doors and windows. He can't see any signs of an alarm system. Gabor probably assumes the dog is enough.

Peter picks the lock on the back door and breathes a sigh of relief when he hears no alarm. He enters and looks around. The first room, in the back of the house, is the kitchen. He opens drawers, looks in cabinets, and scans the fridge. For what? He's not sure. Something that would indicate Gabor has bad intentions. He continues through the remainder of the house, following the same pattern when he finally reaches the bedroom. It looks like Gabor might have been a little late this morning. The rest of the house, including the kitchen, was spotless. But the bedroom is a mess. The bed is unmade, and clothes are scattered all over the floor. A pile of cash sits on top of the dresser, and the two drawers are pulled out and nearly empty. Peter finds a binder in the dresser's top drawer. He opens it, and several photographs fall to the floor.

He sees a familiar face as he bends down to pick them up. She isn't posing for the camera. They're candid shots taken without her knowledge. She was in the restaurant. Peter would recognize the bar anywhere. As he flips through the pages, he finds more disturbing information. Zsuzsa's home address, phone number, regular work schedule, and names of her closest friends and family are typed on a sheet of paper. Kata is included, along with her address, phone number, and everything, including her shopping habits. Either Gabor is so obsessed with her that he's been stalking her, or his interest isn't what he claims. Peter removes his camera from his jacket and snaps several pictures.

He puts the file back and continues around the room. After the bedroom, he checks the bathroom. He finds nothing out of the ordinary. Nothing that might link Gabor to the traffickers. When he's finished, he looks around the house, ensuring he's not left any evidence of his intrusion. While back in the kitchen, he hears something in the front of the house. He creeps to the window and looks out, staying hidden. He sees nothing, then realizes what's missing. The dog is no longer lying on the driveway. Where did he go? He crosses the interior of the house and looks out the back window. He sees the dog squatting on the back lawn. He knew he didn't put enough medication in that sandwich. But he didn't want to hurt the dog. He only wanted him to sleep for a couple hours.

What to do? He looks around the house but can't come up with anything. He's going to have to run for it. The dog's in the backyard. If he runs out the front door, the dog will have to be faster than he is getting to the gate and climbing over. Peter walks to the front door, unlocks it, opens it, and pokes his head out. The dog is still in the back. He shuts the door as quietly as possible, walks down the steps, then heads toward the front gate. When he sees movement out of the corner of his eye, he starts running. He hears the growl behind him. When Peter reaches the gate and springs onto it, the dog is directly behind him. Peter pulls himself to the top and looks down. The dog crashes into the gate and nearly knocks off Peter. The dog slobbers and growls as it jumps to bite him. Peter pulls his leg out of the way and drops on the other side. His knees scream at him in protest. Peter turns around and looks at the dog as it gnashes its teeth and growls, foam dropping from its mouth. As nonchalantly as possible, Peter limps across the street, opens the van door, and gets in. He starts the van, puts it in gear, and pulls away. As he passes the house and the snarling dog, he looks at the front door and sighs. He left it unlocked. He had no choice, but if Gabor comes home and enters through the front, he'll likely know someone has been inside. There's nothing Peter can do about that now.

Chapter Nineteen

Director Toth

Past

We've been at the bar for two hours, and I wonder how much longer these guys will go. This isn't me. I've never been the type to socialize. I liked sports and played football all through my younger years, but otherwise, I kept to myself. Kids would have parties, and sometimes I'd be invited, but I never went. I preferred to stay home. That's why tonight is so out of character for me. I'm in a bar with five other Ministry of the Interior agents, pretending to have a good time.

Juhasz puts an arm around me. "Toth, it's good to have you here. I'm glad you joined us."

"I know. I can't believe I haven't come before."

They all laugh and nod. The agent sitting across from me, Balogh, says, "We wondered about you, Toth. Who goes home to their wife and kid every night? This is why you work for the Ministry, for the perks."

I laugh along with them. I guess it's true what the captain said.

With his arm still around me, Juhasz says, "What do you think, Comrades? Should we show him a really good time?"

They all smile and nod to one another. Juhasz stands, and the rest of them follow. I stumble to my feet. I'm not used to drinking this much, and my head feels like it's floating. We leave and pile into a couple cars. Juhasz drives one and tells me to take the front seat.

When we're on the road, I say, "Hey, I noticed we didn't pay for our drinks. What's the arrangement there?"

He laughs and looks behind me to Balogh in the back seat. "We never pay when we go there. The owner gives us free booze, and we look the other way when his tax notices come due. It's a good arrangement on both sides."

I'm not surprised. This kind of thing happens all the time. We always help "true patriots." Those loyal to the party. We're only in the car for a couple minutes when we pull up beside a small apartment building in Kispest. Juhasz shuts off the engine, and we all get out and walk up to the entrance. Juhasz pushes open the door, and we spill inside. The room looks similar to the bar we just left. But there are differences. This one features a big man standing just inside. He looks at Juhasz, and they nod to each other. We walk a little further into the building, and now I see how this one is different. A stage is in the corner with a woman dancing on it. She's wearing a red bustier and fishnet stockings with heels that look impossible to walk in, let alone dance. Several men sit at tables around the room. Juhasz notices me watching the girl and laughs.

"Now you see what you've been missing, Toth."

I look at him and smile. He motions with his head, and we all sit at a table near the stage. Juhasz calls out to the dancing girl, and she smiles and waves. A new girl, wearing a skimpy blue negligee, approaches and asks us what we want to drink. The other guys request vodka, and I order a beer.

Balogh leans in my ear and says, "A new girl comes out every couple minutes. If you like one, tell our waitress, and head up the stairs. She'll be waiting for you in a bedroom."

I turn and look at him, and he laughs at the expression on my face.

"Yep. We told you you'd have a good time."

The dancing girl disappears behind the stage, and another comes out wearing a white robe. Her blond hair bounces along her shoulders as she prances around. Juhasz bumps me with his elbow. My attraction to her must be apparent.

"You like blondes, huh?"

I turn and look at him, and he waves to our waitress. She comes over, and Juhasz says, "Our buddy here is new. He likes her."

I stare at this interaction, feeling the heat rise in my cheeks. I don't think I can do this.

The waitress smiles and winks at me, then tells me to head up the stairs. She motions to the girl on the stage, and she disappears behind the curtain. The guys slap me on the back and rear as I stand. I can hear them yelling, admonishing me not to be too quick as they laugh. The stairs are close to the door we entered through, and I consider bolting, but then the line from the captain sounds in my ears: "If you want to move up, you have to be all in. Not just at work." I look at the large man standing at the door. He extends his palm toward the stairs.

I pause, consider for a moment, then make my choice. I climb the stairs and wonder where my ascension will end.

Chapter Twenty

Zsuzsa

"When was the last time you went up to the castle?" Gabor asks. He turns the wheel of his red BMW. We've just left dinner and settled into the plush leather seats.

"Umm...I can't remember. It's been a long time."

"Me too. The weather's so nice tonight. What do you think? Want to go? Walk around a bit?"

I'm wearing jeans, a blue blouse, and conservative-heeled sandals. I wouldn't want to hike in this outfit, but a casual walk might be nice. "Okay."

He winks and smiles, and I wonder what he's up to. We're headed west through Pest, and like always, he's singing along to the radio. Not particularly well. He seems especially excited tonight. Before long, we cross the river on the Elizabeth Bridge and turn north toward the castle. At the base of the hill the castle sits on, there's a large roundabout and a tunnel that takes you to the backside of the mountain. I wonder how he plans to reach the top and quickly realize he intends to drive. After he pays the toll and we pass through the gated area, he drives the remaining distance to the top and finds a place to park.

"Let's start at Fisherman's Bastion."

He takes my hand, and we walk along the cobblestone streets. It's March, and although the days are getting longer, the sun has mostly set behind the Buda Hills. There's still plenty of light in the sky, but it'll be fully dark before long.

I think back to the last time I was up here, maybe ten years ago. I came with the guy I was dating at the time. It was different then. It didn't look like it does now. It felt dirty and old. The contrast to today is remarkable. Now, there's a light pole every few feet. Everything is clean and new. We reach the large white gothic church, named after King Matthias, and stare up at it. As a kid, I thought it was named after the saint. I learned the truth when I was a teenager. It features a tall tower on the southeast corner near the entrance adorned with gargoyles.

Gabor looks around, then back at the church. "Have you ever been inside?" he asks, staring at the tower.

I shake my head, and he leads me to the entrance. He tries the door, and it opens.

Inside, there's a vast room with rows of benches and an ornate organ. The tall, arched ceiling is lovely. We walk around looking at all the alters and candles, then exit. It's full dark now, and there's a slight nip to the air. Gabor puts his arm around me, and we walk toward Fisherman's Bastian. Before we reach it, we stop to look at the massive statue of King István, the first king of Hungary. The large copper king sits atop his horse, holding a double cross, reflecting his belief that Hungary could never survive in Europe without embracing Christianity. He became the first Hungarian Christian king and ushered in Catholicism.

In the past, when I've come, the area is crowded with people. I haven't been here in years, but I'm surprised to find we're alone. This is one of the hottest tourist attractions in the whole country, not to mention Budapest. We climb the white steps of Fisherman's Bastian and gaze out over the edge. The view is breathtaking. Across the river is the Parliament Building, Saint Stephen's Basilica, and the rest of Pest. Below us is a beautiful view of the Chain Bridge. Gabor brings me close, and I feel the warmth of his body against mine as we stare at the panoramic view.

"Do you know why seven turrets are here on the Bastian?"

I shake my head, engrossed in the view.

"They represent the seven Hungarian tribes that founded the country before István became king."

I look up at him. "Thank you, Professor. Anything else you'd like to teach me tonight?"

He looks at me, and we both laugh. He leans down and kisses me, and I kiss him back. After a few seconds, we turn back to the city below, comfortable in each other's embrace.

"Okay, I promise not to spout any other interesting facts. But I do have a question."

"Okay."

He releases me, and I'm surprised to see him step back and then take a knee. He pulls a small box from his jacket. It takes a second for me to realize what he's doing, and my heart begins to pound.

"Zsuzsa, I've loved our time together over the last few months. You're all I think about. I want to be with you always. Will you marry me?"

He opens the small box, and a beautiful princess-cut diamond sits atop a white-gold band. I look at the ring, then into his eyes. I've dreamed of this since I was a little girl. In fact, when I was a little girl, I had imagined this man, Gabor, would be proposing marriage to me. It's something I've always wanted. But it feels wrong as I gaze at the ring and at him. I'm not overcome with joy like I thought I would be. Is this because of Peter? Because of what he said?

Gabor senses my hesitation. "Zsuzsa, my family has access to a beautiful chateau in the French Rivera. We can be there in just a few days. We can get married there and stay for our honeymoon. It's gorgeous. You're going to love it. What do you say?"

My head spins as I look at him. He wants to leave? What about my job? None of my friends and family would be at the wedding. Why can't we be married here?

He winces, and I realize he's been on his knee for a long time.

I reach to help him up. As he stands, he holds the box out to me.

"I'm sorry, but can I think about it?"

His face falls.

"I'm not saying no. I just need some time. I wasn't expecting this, and it's quite a shock." I see the disappointment in his eyes and rush to say, "A good shock," and place my hand on his chest. "I just need a day to think about it. I'm sure you didn't rush to this decision. Give me the same courtesy."

He looks away from me and closes the box, putting it back in his jacket pocket. "Okay, but I put a deposit down on that place. I can give you a day. I need to know by tomorrow."

Chapter Twenty-One

Director Toth

Present

I lay on my bed, watching the clock. In five minutes, I'll open the window, climb out of the house, and leave. I've meticulously planned tonight. There isn't a scenario I haven't considered or strategized for. Tomorrow, Rákosi Gyula will no longer be a threat. The time passes, and I slip out of the house. My wife, Eszter, is fast asleep on the couch. She won't wake until morning, having succumbed to her drink-induced coma. When she wakes, I'll be back home in bed, and she'll be none the wiser.

She's disappointed, but I can't help that. We were scheduled to attend a banquet tonight. She loves dressing up and going out. She's been looking forward to it for weeks, but I had to make alternate plans. My excuse was illness. I pretended to have the stomach flu. I'm no trained thespian, but I have to say, my performance was convincing. At one point, I had to tone it down when she and my daughter began to insist on my visiting a doctor. Once I convinced them I'd be okay, Eszter began hitting the bottle, and I knew I'd be in the clear. The only possible hitch in my plans now would be if my daughter were to come check on me. It's a mild concern. She's a teenager, after all.

I finish the five-minute walk, find the car, reach above the passenger tire, and brush the taped key. The angle makes the removal difficult, but I get it free. I pop the trunk, remove the disguise, and climb into the back seat. Corsa's are tiny, especially the hatchback style, like this one. It's a struggle to change my outfit. I'm grateful the location is so remote. Finally, my loungewear has been replaced with a suit and tie. I climb into the front seat, put on the wig, and start the car. It's a fifteen-minute drive, and I can't help checking myself in the mirror at red lights. I look ridiculous. Anyone who knows the man I'm impersonating will quickly see it's not him. I'll have to keep my head down and ensure people don't get a clear view.

When I get close, I find a parking spot two blocks away. I walk to the banquet hall and see a woman standing inside the doors. I don't recognize her and doubt she'd recognize me, but I can't take that chance. I walk around to the kitchen entrance and find the door propped open. I poke my head inside. There are four people, including the chef. None are looking in my direction. They all have their hands full preparing food. I walk past them into the hallway, and they never look up.

Prior to this week, I hadn't been in this building for years. I was confident I could still remember the layout, but to cross all my *t*'s and dot all my *i*'s, I visited. I walked the entire building with a specific plan in mind. With that perspective, I readied myself should anything go wrong, and I get in a pinch.

I finish crossing the secluded hallway, reach the stairs, and ascend. The banquet's being held on the second floor, and when I reach it, I don't hesitate, keeping my head down. I continue up another flight of stairs before reaching my destination. The level should be vacant, except it's not. A woman in a blue dress paces the hallway, talking on a mobile phone. I stop before she looks at me and retreat several steps. I know her. She's Lakatos Noémi, head of the Democratic Coalition. If she sees me, she'll know me even with this ridiculous wig. I retreat to the bottom level, step into an empty room, and look at my watch. I'm fifteen minutes early. I hope he follows his recent pattern of being late. Otherwise, I'll have to resort to plan B.

Tonight's banquet is a fundraiser masquerading as a recognition night for victims of violent crime, including rape. When I became "deathly ill," I called Rákosi Gyula and asked him to stand in my place. Gyula has no idea I invited a man who had previously threatened him. Gyula worked on a case several years ago and later testified against the presumed criminal. He accused the man of raping and killing a young woman in József-város, a district here in Budapest. The man was seen leaving the area several minutes after the murder and knew the young woman. Gyula found other circumstantial evidence and built a case against him, passing it along to the district attorney. The attorney had Gyula testify, and the man was convicted to life in prison. He spent seven years incarcerated until DNA evidence exonerated him. Gyula was at the prison when he was released and apologized to the man. He wasn't in a forgiving mood and told Gyula, "You took seven years of my life. Someday, I'm going to return the favor." Many witnesses heard the interaction, and a file was created. Today, the man will have his revenge. He just doesn't know it yet.

I look at my watch. Ten minutes have passed. I've got to go.

I leave the room and ascend the stairs, keeping my head down. When I reach the floor of the designated meeting spot, I sigh in relief. She's gone. I enter the small meeting room with seven round tables and chairs. I cross the floor to the back table and sit with my back to the door.

Gyula should be entering at any time. I had my associate slip him a note from the threatening man. Surely, they saw each other already and know the other is present in the banquet. The message asks Gyula to come to this room to "bury the hatchet." The note claims the man has forgiven him. A similar note was given to the exonerated man claiming to be from Gyula. The note promises Gyula is stricken with guilt and has developed a plan to compensate him for his time in prison. That note directed him to the first floor ten minutes later than Gyula's. When the former prisoner arrives, he'll find another note guiding him here.

I hear the pop of the door latch as it opens behind me.

"István?" Gyula asks.

I remain still.

Gyula approaches and repeats the name of the man he expects to meet. Finally, he reaches the table and steps in front of me. He peers down at me, although I'm almost as tall as he is sitting. I smile as our eyes lock and his widen, and I raise the gun from beneath the table and fire a bullet into his chest. His eyes go wide with shock as he falls backward. I know I've only got seconds before he dies and minutes before István arrives. I stand and lean over him, seeing his eyes focused on me.

"You should have been honest with me, Gyula."

He tries to speak, but his words are nothing more than a mumble.

"The girls you're hiding will be next."

He frowns and exhales his final breath. Blood oozes from his chest and back and covers the floor around him. I make sure not to touch it as I reach inside his pockets and find the note. I remove it, place the gun on the floor beside him, and leave the room.

Chapter Twenty-Two

Peter

Peter exits the streetcar and walks until he sees the internet café. He enters and notices a different person is sitting behind the desk. He looks around and sees several open computers.

"I'll take an hour, please."

The young man stands, accepts his money, and points to a computer in the middle of the room. There are ten computers in total, and only three are occupied. A lot fewer than the last time he was here when investigating the professor in the international business school. After he logs in, Peter opens Internet Explorer and types "Toth József Újpest." Not surprisingly, there are a lot of men who share that same name. In Hungarian, Toth means Slovak. It's as common a last name as Jones in America. Imagine typing the name Joseph Jones in the United States. The search results would be endless. After twenty minutes, Peter finally has the correct Toth József narrowed down, including known addresses. After another twenty minutes, he has two sheets of notes littering his notepad. Toth was the only child of Tibor and Magdalena. Both parents died in 1955, when Toth was young. His next known address is eight years later in Újpest. No way to know how long he lived there. Peter found the address on his military-registration card. Toth entered the military and was advanced in rank twice. His military service ended after he was wounded in a battle in Czechoslovakia fighting to put down an uprising against the communist regime. After that, he worked for the Ministry of Internal Affairs before moving on to the Hungarian National Police.

Peter leans back in his chair and checks the clock. He only has ten minutes left. Why did the woman in Újpest tell Zsuzsa to investigate her family? What link is there between her and Director Toth? Is there one? According to everything he has read, Toth had no surviving family after his parents died. She couldn't be a sibling. Cousin, maybe? The only link is Újpest.

Peter changes tactics and types, "Sándor Ágota." Another extremely common name, like Agatha Alexander in English. He rushes to locate the correct woman in the time remaining. When he finds her, he checks the lower-right section of the screen and realizes he's only got a minute left before he's logged out. He writes the URL on his notepad, then walks over to the guy behind the desk.

"Can I get more time on the computer?"

The kid looks at him, then at the clock. "Sorry, man, we close in fifteen minutes. I can only sell you time in thirty-minute increments. You'll have to come back tomorrow."

"What if I'm willing to pay for thirty minutes and only get the fifteen before you close?"

The kid looks at him, then shrugs, and Peter hands him enough forints to cover thirty minutes. He walks back to the computer and impatiently strums his fingers as he waits for the machine to load. It's another couple minutes before he reaches the site he had before. The woman is married with two kids. She took her husband's name when she wed. Her husband has another address and may not be living with her anymore. Her maiden name is Horváth. She's the oldest of two. She has a brother. Her mother was also named Ágota, but she died five years ago.

"Everyone, please shut down your computers. We're closing."

Peter looks around. The other two people in the room are logging out, and he'll soon be alone. He needs five more minutes. He looks at the screen and considers the two last names, Sandor and Horváth. Neither surname means anything to him. An idea pops into his mind, and he searches the page for the deceased girl's grandmother.

"Hey, man, sorry. You have to leave now. Shut down your computer." Peter holds up a finger, not taking his eyes from the screen. "Hey, look, I have to go. Come on. Shut it down."

The girl's grandmother was Németh Ágota. Peter frantically reads the screen when the man reaches over him and pushes the power button. "I'm not kidding. You have to go."

Peter glares at him, stands, and walks out. He strolls along Váci Utca, barely noticing the shops closing all around him. He was expecting to see the name of Toth somewhere in his research but didn't. Nothing even close. Frustrated, He shakes his head as he considers the names Sandor, Horváth, and Németh. None mean anything to him. He takes a few more steps, then stops. A family of three trail him and nearly run up his back with his abrupt halt. They split and move around him as he looks at the ground.

The mayor of Újpest is named Németh László. Németh is a prevalent last name. Could that be the link? She's related to the mayor of Újpest, a close friend of Director Toth? Peter's not sure, but he knows he might have found a critical piece.

Chapter Twenty-Three

Director Toth

Present

Walking down the hall toward my office, I notice Erzsi watching me. When I draw close, she points to my door and says, "He's already inside." I push away the annoyance I feel. She knows better than to allow anyone into my office without my permission. I should have locked the door. I typically do. I left earlier in a rush.

I enter the office and find Fekete Balázs, interim head of the major-crimes unit, sitting in the chair opposite my desk. "Balázs," I say, and he stands.

"Sorry, sir. Your secretary said I could wait for you here."

"It's fine." I hang my coat on the rack near the window, then sit behind the desk. "What have you learned?"

He has a file and flips it open. He looks down at it, then back up at me. "What do you know?"

I glare back at him. "What does that mean?"

His voice changes to apologetic. "Oh, I didn't mean...I meant to ask what information you already have. I don't want to tell you things you already know. That's all."

His hand trembles as he holds the file, and I smile inwardly. "Tell me everything. I'll let you know if anything is redundant."

He nods and looks down at the file. "Well, Gyula was at the banquet yesterday filling in for you." He looks back up with a concerned face. "Are you okay, sir?" He mimes a rub on his belly.

I smile and wave a hand. "Oh, yes. It looks like it was just a twenty-four-hour thing. I'm fine, thank you."

He nods and looks back down. "At some point during the banquet, he left the hall and went upstairs to a vacant meeting room. We aren't sure why. He was seen by a woman as he went up the stairs. She estimates the time to be eight twenty-four p.m. He wasn't seen again until eight minutes later, at eight thirty-two p.m., when Detective Varga found him in the room with a gunshot wound to the chest. His presumed killer was kneeling over him when Varga entered. Varga heard a gunshot while in the bathroom below. She deployed her weapon and subdued the man until reinforcements arrived. He was unarmed, but a handgun was on the floor. Ballistics confirms this gun was the murder weapon, registered to the man found with Gyula."

"What do we know about the murderer? Why did he kill him?"

"Long story. Seems Gyula put him in prison for something he didn't do. He was accused of rape and murder, and DNA evidence exonerated him seven years after incarceration. Looks like the guy never forgave him."

"Hmm. So, you've got a motive also. It sounds like there's no question, he's guilty."

"Right. You couldn't frame someone that perfectly. He's guilty. Claims he isn't."

"I want this guy to burn for this. Gyula was one of our own. We need to send a message here. By the way, I've asked for Gyula's computer and files to be brought to me. I know that's unusual, but I want to look at them myself. This one is personal. I'll let you know if I find anything that might help you with other cases."

He gives me a curious look but says nothing. I stand and walk him to the door, patting him on the shoulder before he leaves. "Balázs, it'll be good to work closer with you. Like I told Gyula, my door is always open. I like to be informed of any developments. If you learn anything new, don't hesitate to tell me."

He promises he will and leaves. I close the door, return to my desk, and pick up the phone. I dial the number.

"Sir?"

"I want you to go to Gyula's house. Turn the thing upside down. Tell his wife it's a common procedure after a cop is murdered. We've got to find where he was hiding those girls."

"You got it, Boss."

"How's the other thing?"

"He should know by tonight."

"How do you think it's going to play out?"

"He's pretty confident."

"Good."

I hang up and hear a knock at my door. When it opens, Erzsi stands there with a box in her hands. "Sir, Gyula's files are here. His computer also."

"Excellent. Put them on the table. Set up the computer. I'll take it from there."

Chapter Twenty-Four

Director Toth

Past

"Toth."

I look up from my desk to see the captain standing over me.

"The deputy director wants to see you."

"The director?"

"No...the deputy director. He heard about what you did yesterday. He wants to congratulate you."

"Now?"

"Yes, now. Go up to his office; he's waiting."

The captain walks back to his office as I go to the restroom. Once inside, I examine myself in the mirror. A professional look is an obsession of mine. I never wear a loose-fitting uniform. I make sure my shirts are crisp and wrinkle-free. Appearance is important. Sloppiness of dress reveals a character flaw. I pull my comb from my back pocket and smooth what little hair I have left. I'm not sure I'll need the comb much longer. My hairline is receding at an accelerated pace. I'm warming to the idea of shaving it clean.

Exiting the restroom and walking down the hall, I remind myself to stand up straight. If there's one thing I learned from my years in the military, men of authority appreciate good posture. I work in department one, the investigation division, and the deputy director's office is two stories higher. When I arrive at his office, his secretary looks at me but continues her work. She's a plump woman with black hair and dark lipstick. She smokes a cigarette while typing. She puts it in her mouth, types a line, and removes it with her left hand while keeping her right on the typewriter.

"Can I help you?"

"Yes, I was told to come and meet with the deputy director. He's waiting for me."

"What's your name?"

"Agent Toth."

She picks up her phone and pushes a button on the box next to it. "There's an agent, Toth, here to see you."

The deputy director says something to her on the other end of the line.

"I'll send him in." She looks at me after setting down the phone. "He's expecting you."

I feel a pounding in my chest as I push open the door and enter. The deputy director is sitting behind his desk, smoking a cigar. When he sees me, he stands and comes around with his right hand extended, the cigar in his left. "Comrade Toth, good to see you. Have a seat."

I sit on the chair opposite the desk as he chooses the chair next to me. He opens a small wooden box on the desk and pushes it toward me.

"Cigar?"

I don't smoke, but I'm not about to tell him that. I select one and cut off the tip while he gives me a light. Once I have it going, he leans back in his chair, and I follow suit, doing my best not to cough.

"So, József, do you mind if I call you József?"

"Of course not, sir."

"Tell me about yesterday."

"It was nothing, sir. I think I'm getting too much credit."

"Hmm, that's not what I heard. Tell me what happened from your perspective."

"Okay, well, we brought in the suspect. He's been living in our country for a few months, but we don't know what he's been doing. His papers said he came to the country for work, but from all reports, he wasn't working much."

"He's American?"

"Yes."

He waves at me to continue.

"We brought him in for routine questioning. He's supposed to be working on a new telephone system. I started asking him questions, and I didn't like his behavior. He seemed too perfect. It's like he was coached. If I were a foreigner brought in by the police of another country for questioning, even if I had nothing to hide, I'd be nervous. But this guy wasn't. Something wasn't right. The more I questioned him, the more I knew it. Once we applied some pressure, he started to talk."

He laughs and leans forward, slapping my shoulder. "Turns out, this guy is an American spy. We've already learned a lot from him. You did well, József. Very good."

"Thank you, sir."

"That brings me to why I wanted to see you. Did you know you were almost never hired here?"

"No."

He nods and puffs on his cigar. "Yep, you very nearly never passed the background check."

That catches me by surprise. I've been nothing but loyal to the country and the party. There's nothing in my background at all questionable.

"I can see that surprises you. No idea why?"

"No, sir."

"Your father."

"My father?"

He nods, and his eyes turn cold.

"Sir, my father is the mayor of Újpest. He's a loyal patriot."

He shakes his head. "I'm not talking about your adoptive father. I'm talking about your biological one."

Now I understand. "Sir, I haven't seen that man since I was a small child. I have nothing to do with him."

I feel the penetrating stare of his unblinking eyes. "He was put to death. A traitor. An enemy to the state."

This doesn't come as a surprise. I had suspected this.

"I've never really trusted you, József. Since you were hired, you've been tested. Nobody is completely trusted around here, but you were under a microscope. To your credit, you've passed. You've proven yourself worthy of a new assignment. We need true patriots like you."

I'm not sure what to say. "Thank you, sir."

He stands and extends his hand. "Carry on with your current assignment until you hear from me. I'll be in touch."

I take his hand, thank him, and leave the room. Walking down the hall, I no longer need to remind myself to stand up straight.

Chapter Twenty-Five

Detective Szabo

I extend my hand and tap on the door. Nothing happens. I look at Erzsi. She's got the phone held to her ear, and she mouths, "Harder." I sigh, and this time, I use my knuckles.

"Come," is the muffled command on the other side of the door.

I push open the door and step inside. He's seated at his desk, looking at a file of papers. He looks up, his reading glasses perched on the end of his nose, his eyes questioning.

"Sir, can I talk to you for a minute?" I've already taken several steps toward him and closed the door.

He looks at the clock on the wall and then back to the papers on his desk.

"Can it wait?"

"Oh...yeah, sure. Sorry." I turn to leave, feeling both relief and disappointment.

"Wait...Szabo, I can give you five minutes. It's now or never. I won't have any time later. What's this about?"

I turn back to face him. I almost chicken out, then decide it's too important not to go forward. "Sir, it's about Gyula."

His eyebrows shoot up, and he motions to the chair across the desk. I take the seat.

"What about Gyula?"

Since I heard the news about his murder, I've known I should talk to the director about what I saw. I just don't know how to start.

Toth sees my hesitation. "What is it, Szabo?"

"Sir, I think we have the wrong man in custody for Gyula's murder."

"What?" His voice is stern as he glares at me. "I don't have time for this, Detective. That man threatened Gyula and was found at the scene of the murder with blood on his hands. The gun belonged to him. How can you say we have the wrong man?"

"Okay, maybe he did kill Gyula. But there's more to it than that. He was working with someone."

Toth frowns and takes off his glasses. "Who?"

"Detective Farkas."

"What?"

"I saw Farkas and Gyula meet at Heroes' Square two days ago. They didn't know I was watching. Gyula must have learned who Farkas is and confronted him about it. He must have threatened to tell you, and Farkas had him killed."

Toth extends his palm toward me and exhales. "Wait, you were following them and saw them meet, and because of this, you think Farkas killed him?"

"I wasn't following both of them, only Farkas."

"Why?"

"Because he's a trafficker. He's giving inside information to the organization."

"How do you know that?"

I told him about my conversation with Peter in jail. About how Peter was convinced there was a mole in the task force and that Kovacs knew who it was, then was killed.

"Detective, do you remember what you told me after Kovacs's murder?"

I look down and nod.

"You said that Peter killed Kovacs. That you were convinced he was working with the traffickers. You pointed out how his wife was murdered. You also said he was the one who found Andras, the restaurant owner, then killed him. Then he went to Ukraine when nobody else knew the girls were taken there. You convinced me to arrest him. Remember?"

I look away. "Sir, I was wrong." He exhales and leans back in his chair.

"Szabo, I don't know what to believe at this point. But I can tell you, I don't believe Peter. The trafficking has stopped, and Peter is in New York. That just shows he was involved. Now stop wasting my time accusing your colleagues of serious crimes and get back to finding the girls the traffickers have taken."

"But, sir—"

He points to the clock on the wall. "Your five minutes are up. Get out of my office."

I stand and leave the room. I walk down the hall, through the bullpen of cubicles, and enter my office. I sit in my chair and look at my team but focus on one member. I don't care what Toth says. Farkas did it. He killed another cop—actually, more than one. Anger boils in me as I stare at the back of Farkas's head. He's guilty, and I'm going to prove it.

Chapter Twenty-Six

Peter

Peter parks the white Volkswagen van along the street next to the park and looks at a bench. He smiles, seeing his friend seated smoking a cigarette. Peter exits the van and walks across the grass. Tom looks over.

"Well...if it isn't the most intelligent man I know."

Peter nearly falls over with surprise and checks over his shoulder to see if anyone is behind him. He sits down on the bench and gives his friend a curious look.

Tom puffs out a breath of smoke and smiles. "I've been banished from the apartment. My wife says I should start saying the opposite of what my instincts tell me. You're my guinea pig. What do you think?"

Peter rolls his eyes and puts his arm over the back rail of the bench. "Have you ever seen the movie *Grumpy Old Men*?"

Tom eyes him and shakes his head.

"You should watch it. I think you'd enjoy Walter Matthau's character."

"I'll see what I can do to find a copy."

"Let me know."

"I will."

"Have you talked with your sister? How's Lili?"

"Fine. Safe. She's pretty bored."

"I bet."

"She keeps asking when she'll be able to leave. She wants to hear from you."

"I'll call her. I need more evidence, though. Until I have it, she isn't safe. Speaking of, that's why I'm here."

Tom takes another drag on his cigarette and puffs it into the air. "You're the smartest and most capable man I know. It would be an honor to help you."

Peter chuckles. "Okay, okay. As capable as I may be, I can't be everywhere at once. I need another set of eyes, and since you're so good at sitting on your butt, I thought of you."

"Doing what?"

"I need you to follow someone."

"Who?"

"Zsuzsa."

"The bartender?"

"Yep."

"Based on your descriptions of her, I'd love to. But why?"

"She's been dating a guy I don't trust. I worry about her but can't spend all my time watching her. Plus, it would be better if she doesn't know I'm following her. She won't recognize you if she sees you."

"Is she truly in danger, or is this jealousy?"

"Probably both. But the circumstances surrounding their meeting seem too convenient. I never believed it was by accident. So, I kinda broke into his house and looked around." Peter shows him the photos he took while inside Gabor's home.

"Wait, is that Zsuzsa?" Tom points to a picture of a picture of her. It's not super clear, but it's passable.

"Yes."

Tom lets out a low whistle, then breaks into a coughing fit. When he can talk again, he says, "You weren't kidding about her. She went on a date with you?"

"Is this you saying the opposite of what you think? Or did you forget that?"

Tom holds up the picture to get a better look. "I'm sorry. I meant to say, this repulsive woman went on a date with you? How lucky she was that you were even interested?"

Peter chuckles. "All right. Yes, she's gorgeous and out of my league. Anyway...did you look at the rest?"

"Yes. It would seem he's quite interested in Zsuzsa. He's either a stalker, or he has bad intentions."

"Exactly. Until I know which, I need you to help me by watching her."

"Okay, I can do that. Does this include peering at her through the window of her apartment? Maybe making sure she's safe in the shower?"

Peter laughs. "No, you dirty old man. Outside her building will be fine."

"Hmm, pity." He continues looking at the picture of Zsuzsa. "So, what will you be investigating while Zsuzsa and I spend time together?"

"I told you about the girl who was taken and murdered in Újpest, right? The one who wasn't reported missing for a week?"

"Right."

"Zsuzsa talked to her mother. She wouldn't say much but told Zsuzsa to look into the woman's family. I did that and found something exciting."

"Yeah?"

"Her brother is the mayor of Újpest."

Tom looks up at Peter. "Really?"

"Yep. Their family has a long history of organized crime in Budapest, dating back to communist days."

"So why did they kill the girl?"

"I'm not sure. That's what I need from the mother. Maybe she doesn't even know, but I need to try and talk to her."

"So, the mayor of Újpest is dirty?"

"Maybe. But there's something more. I just need to find out what it is."

Chapter Twenty-Seven

Zsuzsa

I hate grocery shopping. In fact, I think I'd rather have a tooth pulled. It's funny because I love to shop for everything else—clothes, home décor, beauty products. But I *hate* getting groceries. Maybe it's so many years of working around food in a restaurant. It's a chore, something I have to do as a responsible adult. I'll go weeks without groceries. When I opened my fridge this morning, I knew I couldn't avoid it any longer. The milk was expired, and I was out of eggs. I love eggs. They're the only thing that really gets me to come here.

I stand in the produce section, staring at a rack of tomatoes, and wonder where they all came from. How can there be so many varieties? Roma, Campari, cherry. There are even green ones. I wonder how many people buy different kinds. Or is it like the restaurant? The same people order the same food or drinks almost every time. How many tomatoes are thrown away every day due to spoilage? I pick up one of the green ones and squeeze it. It feels just like the red ones, ripe. It makes me wonder: does it taste different? Like green and red apples? On impulse, I raise it to my mouth and take a big bite. Tomato juice shoots out and oozes from my mouth. It runs down my hand and chin. With it still pressed to my teeth, I look to my right as an old woman stares at me. I smile and shrug. She gives me a disapproving look, which makes me laugh. My boisterous laugh blares in the quiet section. Everybody is looking at me now.

I feel a need to explain myself. "Don't worry. I'm going to pay for it." People continue to watch me. Across the aisle, standing near the onions, is a woman about my age. Our eyes lock, and she pushes her cart toward me.

"Zsuzsa?"

I wipe the tomato juice from my mouth and put the remainder in my cart.

"Zsuzsa? Is that you?"

She knows me, but I don't know her. I don't recognize her at all. "Yep."

"I haven't seen you in forever." She steps around my cart, leaning forward.

Surprised and unsure what to do, I stand awkwardly as she kisses the air on either side of my head, her cheeks brushing mine. When she steps back, I still have no idea who she is.

She says, "You don't know who I am, do you?"

I flash her an embarrassed smile and shake my head.

"It's Barbara. We grew up together in Érd."

As soon as she says it, I can see it. It's been at least fifteen years since I've seen her, and she looks different. Time hasn't been as good to her as her brother. She dies her hair blond, and she shouldn't. It doesn't work with her natural coloring. She's at least thirty pounds heavier than the last time I saw her, and she has wrinkles around her eyes and a crease on her forehead. She looks like she might go to the solarium several times a week. Her skin is unnaturally tan and leathery. Her eyes are still a lovely shade of blue, and her smile is warm and inviting. She was always such a lovely girl, and it troubles me to see her like this.

"Barbara? It's so good to see you." I extend my arms, and we embrace. "What have you been up to? Do you live around here?"

"I do. I just moved in a couple blocks away."

I wonder what Gabor has told her. Does she know I live close by? She must know we're dating.

"That's great. It's been so long. Tell me about yourself. What have you been up to?"

"Oh, I got married and have a couple kids. My tool bag of a husband just split. I guess he didn't like being a father. He still acts like a teenage boy."

"Oh no. I'm sorry. How old are your kids?"

"Little, just five and three. Two girls." She pulls out her purse, rifles through her wallet, and removes a photo. The girls are posed in a photographer's studio. They each have light hair and pretty blue eyes. It's obvious they're sisters, even without the matching outfits. They look so much like their mother did at their ages.

"Oh, how darling. They're so cute."

"Thank you." She stares at the photo for a beat, puts it back in her wallet, and looks at me. Her eyes suddenly fill with tears, and she looks away, brushing at the corners. "I never thought he'd leave. It's been so hard. I just feel all alone."

I feel a rush of sympathy for her and wrap her in my arms. She doesn't just cry; she sobs, her body trembling. I look around and find most people are no longer watching. Those who still are look away under my hard gaze.

After several seconds that feel like minutes, she pulls away and takes a tissue from her purse. "I'm sorry. I just haven't had anyone to talk to. It's nice to have a shoulder to cry on." She smiles and looks at my damp shoulder, then tries to wipe it dry with the tissue. It separates and leaves a white, filmy mess all over my shirt. Realizing she's making it worse, she tries again with her empty hand. "I'm so sorry."

I wave my hand, then brush off my shoulder. "It's fine. Don't worry about it. What about your family? Don't they help you?"

She scoffs. "My family? Yeah, right." She sees my surprise. "My dad's gone. You knew that, I assume? Only my mom and brother are around anymore. I don't talk to them much."

"Why not?"

She eyes me skeptically. "You don't know?"

"Know what?"

She shakes her head. "Hmm, I thought everyone from back home knew. My dad was involved in something illegal. Nobody knows what, and he was never arrested, but he was killed several years ago. It was ruled an accident, but it was no accident. Whatever it was, my mom knew and turned a blind eye. She hasn't spoken of it since. Now, I think my brother's involved."

Her words hit me like a twister, and I know all the color has drained from my face. She looks at me, and our roles have reversed.

"Zsuzsa? Are you okay?"

I put my hand to my head and bend forward, taking in big gulps of air. "I'm sorry. I just got a little lightheaded. I think I was locking my knees."

She helps me to a bench near the front of the store. We sit for a few seconds while I take deep breaths, bent over. Something inside me screams, *I knew it!* He always seemed too good to be true, and here's the proof.

Twenty minutes later, I exit the bus at my apartment's stop. While we sat on the bench in the store, Barbara and I chatted for a few more minutes. It was mostly about her, which was fine by me. In the little she asked about me, it was clear Gabor had never mentioned dating me. I asked about her family, keeping it light but hoping to learn more. Turns out, only half of what Gabor had told me was true. He had been married before, but his wife left him. Barbara thinks she might have learned about his illegal behavior. They never had any kids. He does actually work in advertising, but she thinks it's mostly a front. She didn't know what the illegal activity was but admitted to not really wanting to know.

She may not know, but I do. He's a trafficker. It explains so much. That's why he cared about me going to talk to the woman in Újpest. That's also why he kept asking questions about Peter. I feel so stupid. I trusted him. Did he arrange for me to be followed that night after I left work, knowing he'd be there to save me? He's been playing me this whole time, and I feel used.

As I walk the final distance to my building, I realize I'm supposed to see him tonight. He's expecting to receive my answer about his proposal. I reach my apartment and enter the building. I'm carrying a couple grocery bags, which makes opening the door and calling the elevator a little more difficult, but I manage. When I reach my floor, my heart drops. Gabor is outside my door, and he's looking right at me.

"Szia," he says, smiling and cheerful. He comes toward me, and I want to spit in his face. He leans forward to kiss me, and I stand still, his lips brushing mine. He disgusts me, but I can't show it. When he steps back, I flash him the most enthusiastic smile I can muster.

"Are you okay?" he asks.

"I'd be better if you'd help me with these bags." I push them into his arms, turn away, and fumble with my keys while I think. What am I going to do? I don't want him inside my apartment. I don't want him anywhere near me. I want him out of my life. But I know that can't be. At least not yet. He's dangerous and a liar. I realize I don't even know him. He's been acting with me. I've got to play it cool and think. Be as unreadable as possible.

I open the door, and he follows me in. I tell him I have to go to the bathroom and leave him in the kitchen putting things away. I close the door and stare at myself in the mirror, taking deep breaths. My breathing is erratic, and I force myself to calm down. I can do this. I know I can. I worked with Andras for months. Every day, I was in danger, and I survived. Agoston took me to Ukraine, and I survived that too. But if I'm being honest, I almost didn't. If Peter and Kovacs hadn't come...Peter! I've got to find him. He knew. He warned me about Gabor, and I didn't listen. I thought he was just being jealous. He was right again.

A soft knock on the door.

"Zsuzsa? Are you okay?"

I turn to the closed door. "No, sorry. I'm not feeling well."

"Oh no. What's the matter?"

"I'm sick. I don't know if it's something I ate. I'm not doing very well."

"Do you want me to get you something? Do you need to see a doctor?"

"No. I'll be okay. I just need some time. Sorry, this is kind of embarrassing. I need some time alone."

He's silent for a bit, then says, "Okay. Call me later. Let me know how you're doing."

"I will."

I watch his shadow move away from the door and hear his footsteps in the kitchen. I listen as the exterior door opens and shuts. I look in the mirror and take a deep breath, then open the bathroom door and rush over to the phone. Peter left me a note with his number that I've hidden under the receiver. I push the phone aside and pick up the note. I dial the number and press the receiver to my ear, waiting for the ringing to sound. Before it does, a hand covers my mouth, and I feel something hard and cold pressed to my temple.

"Zsuzsa...Zsuzsa. I'm so disappointed," Gabor whispers in my ear.

Chapter Twenty-Eight

Detective Szabo

He exits the front doors of the building, and I start the engine. He walks as if he has no care in the world. What kind of person can kill another and feel no remorse? No guilt. He disgusts me. Every day, I've looked a trafficker and killer in the eye without knowing it. I follow him as he walks to the parking garage and gets in his car. He takes the same route as the other night, except this time, he turns on his street and parks. He gets out and goes inside. I've got to get in there. There must be evidence inside. He's too clever to leave anything at the office. Maybe he'll leave again tonight, and I'll get my chance.

I turn on the radio and lean back in my seat. Danubius Rádió is playing a song by a Hungarian rock band, Locomotiv GT. I remember not too long ago, all the music on the radio was Hungarian. Now, English is more common than our own language. I let the love song take me, and my mind wanders back to last night. I went to see Zsuzsa. I told her it was because I wondered if she had talked to the woman in Újpest. And yes, it was true. I was curious. But more than that, I wanted to see her. When she saw me sitting at a table alone, she actually smiled. She was pleased to see me. It's the first time she's ever smiled when seeing me. Since leaving the restaurant, that smile hasn't left my mind. I imagine what it might be like to see it daily.

After exchanging pleasantries, I asked her about the mother in Újpest. The question seemed to catch her off guard, and she hesitated. I got the feeling she was debating what to say. She said she couldn't get the woman to talk. But I could tell there was something more to it.

Movement in my rearview mirror pulls me from the memory. Before I can react, someone opens my car door and sits beside me. I reach for my gun, but I'm too late. A gun is pressed to my ear. From the corner of my eye, I see my attacker.

"What are you doing?"

"Stopping you from doing something you'll regret." Peter pulls his gun away.

"You didn't have to hold a gun to my head."

He waves it in his hand. "No bullets." As if my comment reminds him, he empties bullets from his jacket pocket and loads the gun. "Still think I killed Kovacs?" he asks and smiles.

I ignore the question. "How did you get back in the country? You left. I know you did."

He shakes his head. "It wasn't easy. I had to sneak back in." He finishes with his gun, checks the safety, then puts it back in his pocket. "Look, we need to talk. I know what you think, but you're wrong."

I stare at him. "About what?"

"About the mole. About Farkas."

"I see going back to America hasn't changed you. You still think you know everything."

"Are you denying it?"

My silence speaks volumes.

"That's what I thought. Look, I've been following you and Farkas. I know what you think. You think because he met with Rákosi Gyula the other night, he's the one who killed him. Did it ever cross your mind they were working together?"

Working together? "They were both traffickers?"

Peter rolls his eyes and shakes his head. "No...they both knew who the mole was. They were working to expose him."

"They were?"

He nods.

"Who is it?"

"Director Toth."

I laugh. "What? You're kidding."

"I'm not. Think about it. He's got the perfect job for it. He knows everything that happens in the country. He knows what the police are investigating. He even directs what they should investigate. It's like being the detective of your own crime."

I shake my head and look away. Toth? "I don't believe you."

"Okay, then don't. But how plausible is your theory? So, Gyula knows Farkas is a trafficker, but instead of exposing him, he confronts him at Heroes' Square. Then he gives him time to prepare a defense before exposing. That sounds more like a James Bond villain."

I know he's right, but I'm not about to tell him.

"There's a way for you to find out, you know?"

"How?"

"Before Kovacs died, he told me he went to the jail and checked the visitor log. He saw something but was killed before he could tell me what it was. Go look through it, and you'll have your proof."

He moves to exit the car.

"Peter?"

He stops and looks at me.

"Why tell me now?"

"I told you. To stop you from doing something stupid. I also need more allies in this fight. Toth has all the resources on his side."

"There's something else you should know."

"What?"

"I told Toth about Farkas and Gyula meeting at Heroes' Square. I told him I thought Farkas was the mole, and he dismissed it. But he knew they were talking."

He shakes his head and looks up at the car ceiling. "Farkas is in danger. He'll be coming after him." Peter turns back to me and grabs my arm. His voice is forceful. "You've got to keep information from Toth. His power is his connection. He relies on knowing what's being investigated before it is. Keep him in the dark, but don't let him know."

He's out of the car and gone before I can say anything else.

Chapter Twenty-Nine

Renata

After leaving the school, I checked the McDonald's. Zoe wanted to go there when we tested whether anyone would recognize me, and I know she goes there often. I sat down at a table and waited for a while but gave up and left. I went to her apartment next. I knew I couldn't go inside. I stood across the street debating my options. Going in would be a terrible risk, considering the woman who'd claimed to be my sister knows I'm staying with Zoe. I'm sure there is more than one Zoe at the school, but after finding my school and class schedule, I wouldn't be surprised if she located the correct one. I'd worried that she or the big guy could already be inside waiting for us and knew that If I went in, I could end up like before. Shipped off to another country. Or worse, end up like Agnes. I almost walked away, but I knew I couldn't leave Zoe. I had to find her.

I went in. Fortunately, she wasn't there, and neither was anyone else. If someone was watching the building, I didn't see them. I left as quick as I could.

Now I'm back at the school, walking down the hallway, trying to think of where she might be. I come around a corner and stop, ducking back to where I was. A woman is in front of me who matches the professor's description. I peek around the corner and see she's waiting outside the classroom of one of my other professors. She's lean, mid-twenties, with dark-brown hair. She looks like she's in great shape. She could be a student but is too old for the average age. I've never seen her before. But then again, I haven't seen a lot of students here. It's a big school. I better not risk it. I turn around and walk back the other way. I'll look for Zoe elsewhere.

I enter the library and scan the tables. There's a group of six sitting together around a table in the back corner. I breathe a sigh of relief. I can't see her face, but I know the color and cut of her hair. It's Zoe. I hesitate before approaching. Those in the group probably won't recognize me, but I don't want to take any chances, especially with some woman wandering the school asking about me. Zoe's back is to me in the worst position possible. She's facing the wall. No way she'll see me unless she turns around.

I walk over to the table nearest them and sit in the last chair with my back against the wall. If she looks up, maybe I can distract her enough to look in my direction.

Her head's down, and it looks like she's reading a book. The two girls to her left are whispering about something. The two boys across the table are comparing notes. The final member of the group is asleep, face down, and not even trying to hide it.

I sit, staring at Zoe, mentally willing her to look. When she finally does, she joins the girls in whispering. Grr, this isn't working. What if the woman comes in here? I've got to get Zoe's attention. The longer I wait, the more likely we'll be found.

I try a cough. Nothing. I stand up and stretch. The boys look at me, but Zoe doesn't. I can hear some of their whispering and know they're gossiping about another girl. Finally, I can't wait any longer. I walk over to the table and stand by Zoe. The whole table looks at me, except for the slumbering guy. I don't say anything, trying to hide my face from the group. I have several classes with some of them. I lock eyes with Zoe, motioning for her to follow with my head and eyes. I walk away and reach one of the rows of bookcases and disappear inside. Less than a minute later, Zoe joins me.

"What are you doing?" she asks.

I grab her shoulder and pull her deeper into the bookcases. "I'm so glad I found you."

She frowns. "What are you talking about?"

"Someone came looking for me," I whisper.

Surprise registers on her face. "To the apartment?"

"No. To one of my classes. She's still here somewhere."

"No way."

"Way. Professor Takács told me."

"How did you see her?"

"I came to the school. I needed help with some homework. Anyway, it's not important. A woman claiming to be my sister came around asking about me. My sister's twelve. This woman was in her twenties."

"Wow."

"Yeah. And I think she's still here. I saw a woman matching the description in the hallway when I was looking for you."

"Hmm, what do you want to do?"

"I'm not sure."

"Maybe I should go look. See if she's still around."

"You can't."

"Why?"

"Because the professor told her you were picking up my homework. She'll be looking for you too."

She laughs. "She doesn't know what I look like."

"We can't take that chance. She already knew what school I go to and who my teachers are. I bet she can find you too."

"Renata, you're being paranoid."

"You think?"

"Yeah."

"Hmm, maybe I should get Agnes to explain it to you. Oh, wait, she can't because *she's dead*."

We glare at each other, then Zoe's expression changes. "Okay...okay. So what do you want to do?"

"We've got to get out of here. Away from the school. But we've got to be careful."

"I need to get my bag. I'll be right back."

"Don't tell our classmates."

"I won't."

Fifteen minutes later, we're walking away from the school. We never saw the woman but got some strange looks from classmates as we hid and peeked around corners.

"Let's go home," Zoe says. "We'll figure out what to do."

I glare at her. "Do you not even listen? We can't go home."

"Why not?"

"If they know your name, then they'll be able to find where you live. They found Agnes, remember?"

Finally, the enormity of the situation seems to set in. "What are we going to do?"

"We can't go to anyone who knows you. They wouldn't understand."

"Where then? You don't know anyone here. Plus, if they know me and my friends and family, they'll definitely know yours."

We're walking past Gellert Hill and Freedom Bridge. I look at the hotel. I wish we had money. We could stay in a hotel until we find another solution. Panic rises in my chest as I consider how hopeless our situation is.

"Renata, what are we going to do?"

"Dominic."

"What?"

"Dominic will help us."

"The football player? The hot one?"

"Yeah. He got me my diary, remember? He talked to Peter. They didn't know about him."

"Who's Peter?"

"The guy who saved me in Ukraine."

"Oh, right."

I grab her arm.

"Come on. Let's go find Dominic. Maybe he can connect us with Peter."

Chapter Thirty

Peter

Peter sits outside the Tesco on Garam Út and waits. An hour ago, he had walked into the grocery store and took his time, surveying each employee until he found one with the name tag of Ágota. The woman was older than the photo he'd found online, but it was her. Once, while he'd been waiting, she came outside for a smoke break. Seeing her leave the building, he prepared himself to follow. But she'd stepped away, lit a cigarette, and chatted with a coworker. Ten minutes later, she was back inside.

Another thirty minutes pass, and Peter sees her exit the front entrance. She's replaced her red-vest work uniform with a green jacket. Peter follows as she leaves the parking lot and heads down the street. After a five-minute walk, she enters the subway station at Dózsa.

György Út. Peter follows her down the stairs, knowing she'll be headed north toward Újpest-Központ. As they stand on the platform waiting for the train, he surveys the other passengers. None appear to be watching her. The train arrives, and she steps on. Peter joins her in the same car but enters through a different door. At first, he keeps his distance, analyzing each passenger. Once he's sure nobody is paying attention to her, he approaches. He sits beside her, and when she looks up, he smiles. Never in a million years would he be interested. She isn't his type. But he doesn't have any better idea. Their eyes lock, and he winks. A smile plays at the corners of her lips. He can tell she's curious and a bit flattered.

"Szia. I'm Peter." He continues to smile, acting confident.

"Szia."

"How's your day been?"

"Not bad," she says, smiling.

He leans back and sighs. "Yeah, I just got off work."

"Oh yeah? Me too."

"What do you do?" he asks, his voice light and curious.

"You first."

"I'm a high school history teacher."

"Impressive."

"You think?"

"It's better than a grocery-store cashier."

Peter chuckles. "You haven't been around a lot of high school kids. Is that what you do? Cashier?"

She nods. "It's not much, but I'm getting by."

The overhead announcement informs them the next stop will be hers. She looks up, then toward the door.

"Is this your stop?"

She nods, looking disappointed.

"Are you in a hurry?"

She looks back at him, hopefully. "Not really."

"How about a cup of coffee? At the next stop, there's a place outside the subway station."

"Okay."

Until they reach the station, they talk about the weather and where they're from. She asks if he has any kids, and he tells her he doesn't. She tells him she has a daughter.

They exit the subway and walk to the small café. She orders a coffee, and he gets a tea. Once seated at a small table, he says, "Ágota, it wasn't by accident that I came and sat down next to you on the subway."

She looks at him and smiles, blushing. He inwardly groans. That's not what he meant. This is going to be worse than he thought.

"A woman has stopped by your apartment several times asking about your daughter. The older one."

Her smile vanishes, and she looks away, her jaw clenching and unclenching. She strangles her coffee and stands, but Peter reaches out and grabs her hand. "I just want to ask you a few questions, and I'm gone. Nobody will ever know I talked to you." He looks up at her, his hand still on hers. She looks down at him, and he can see she's debating. Finally, she sits.

"You've got five minutes."

They're alone in the café, but Peter keeps his voice low, not wanting the barista to hear. "Why did you not report your daughter missing?"

"You don't beat around the bush."

"I've only got five minutes."

"What do you care? What's your angle?"

Peter explains how he got into this whole thing. About being hired by Kata to investigate Andras, about going to Croatia and Ukraine, and about the job offer with the Hungarian National Police and the trafficking.

She holds up her hand. "Wait, you work for József?"

"No. I did. I know he's the one behind the trafficking in the city. He killed another cop, a friend of mine. He threw me in jail and blamed me for it to shut me up. Long story, but I was able to get out. How do you know him?"

"He's my uncle."

"Your uncle?" Peter can't help the bewilderment in his voice. He looked into both Toth and her family background. There's no link.

"I should say, he's my adopted uncle. His parents died when he was young, and my grandparents took him in."

"So why did he kill your daughter?"

She looks back before answering, making sure they're still alone. "My daughter recognized someone. I'm not sure if it was him or my other uncle."

"The mayor of Újpest?"

She nods. "She was hanging around some older girls from out of town. She was cute and mature for her age. The boys thought she was older. I don't know exactly what happened, but she was in the wrong place and recognized someone. They killed her."

"You knew it was them, but you didn't say anything because of your younger daughter."

Tears flow from her eyes. "I can't lose another. She's all I've got left. I had to leave my family. I couldn't be around it. I went from a wealthy family to nothing. If I lose her..."

Peter reaches across the table and takes her hand. "Let me help you."

"How?"

"I can move you. Put you and your daughter somewhere safe."

She laughs through the tears. "Nobody is safe from them. They can reach anyone. If they knew I was talking to you...I've got to go."

She stands and runs out the door.

An hour later, Peter walks along Váci Utca, headed to his apartment. For a week after returning to Budapest, he'd avoided it, staying in a hotel instead. There was never much inside the living space anyway: a bed, an office, and an empty refrigerator. After a week of surveying, he decided it was safe to stay there again. But he's been very cautious. He leaves the apartment early in the morning and comes back late. None of his neighbors have seen him, and he stays as quiet as a mouse. He reaches the apartment building, checks the stairway for traffic, then enters. Within seconds, he's inside. He doesn't turn on the lights, feeling his way along the hallway until he reaches the study. He closes the door behind him, flips on the lights, and sits at the desk. Because this room has no window, he's confident no one will see the lights on. An unfamiliar buzzing noise emanates from his jacket. Several days ago, he had purchased a mobile phone. Only a few people have the number, and he hasn't received any calls. He pulls out the phone, extends the antenna, and presses the answer button.

"Hello?"

"Peter, it's Tom. They have Zsuzsa."

"What? Who has Zsuzsa?"

"I think it's her boyfriend. They left in a red BMW. He appeared to be taking her at gunpoint. He kept close to her, and she seemed upset but followed his commands."

"Where are you?"

"In Érd. I followed them to a house, then found a pay phone. They haven't left since arriving. I took a chance leaving to call you."

"Give me the address, then go back. Keep an eye on the house, but stay out of sight until I get there."

Chapter Thirty-One

Director Toth

Past

It's been two weeks since the deputy director called me into his office and told me I would get a new assignment. Since then, I've heard nothing from him, until today. He called me and told me to meet him at a bar near our office. I left work a few minutes ago, and now I'm making the five-minute walk to the bar. After talking to the deputy director, I've been pondering two things: first, what will the new assignment be? Second, how did he know about my father?

I reach the bar and enter. It's dark inside, and my eyes take a moment to adjust. A woman approaches and asks if I'd like a spot at the bar. She's pretty, young. I tell her I'm here to meet someone. I scan the bar and tables and see him sitting in the back. He sees me and waves me over. I tell the girl and walk past her.

He's with another man. The man is older, probably in his mid-fifties. I recognize him, although it's been years since I last saw him up close.

When I approach the table, the deputy director motions for me to sit. Neither man stands. I take a seat and find that the woman has followed me over.

"What would you like?"

"Get him vodka," the deputy director says and dismisses her. He turns to me. "József, do you know who this is?"

I wonder if this is a test. Does he know I once covered up the man's murder? If I say I do, will they hold it against me? If I say I don't, will they know I'm lying? Many people know Kossa István, minister of the interior, given his political position. I figure I'm better off keeping my answer simple.

"Yes, sir, I do."

The man stares at me, and I look for some recollection in his eyes but see none. He was rather distraught that night, not to mention drunk.

"Good, then I don't need to explain to you how important a man the minister is."

"No, sir. It's an honor to meet you, Minister."

The man says nothing, still eyeing me.

"Minister Kossa has a special assignment he needs help with. I've recommended you for the job."

"It would be an honor to serve the minister in any way I can, sir."

The deputy director turns to the minister and smiles. "I told you, he's a good soldier. We've tested him. He'll be perfect for you."

I wonder what the assignment might be, but I know better than to ask. My job isn't to ask questions. It's to do as I'm told.

"József, one of my many responsibilities as minister of the interior is to welcome visiting foreign dignitaries. I need someone who can ensure they enjoy their time in our country. Their visits are critical to the country and party. Some wish to sightsee, others to party and have a good time, and most want to enjoy the companionship of females. Your job will be to see that their desires are fulfilled."

"I understand, sir, and would be happy to assist however I can."

"Good. I have a couple houses here in Budapest where gentlemen experience such companionship. I understand you've been to my houses before?"

I didn't know they were his. I began visiting a couple local brothels with my colleagues. "Yes. Thank you, sir."

The minister smiles, and the deputy director laughs and pats me on the back. "I told you he'd be perfect."

The smile vanishes. "József, it's important nobody knows who owns the houses. You'll be my right-hand man. I'll only communicate with you. You'll be responsible for running the houses and caring for the needs of the dignitaries."

"I understand, sir."

The deputy director leans forward. "From all outward appearances, you'll still be working as an agent in the internal affairs. As far as anyone knows, including your captain, you'll be working on a special assignment from me. Nobody is to know about your role with the minister. Understood?"

"Yes, sir."

"Good. Minister, what do you think, another round? Then maybe we can take József to one of your houses to get better acquainted."

Chapter Thirty-Two

Zsuzsa

Consciousness comes to me. My head feels heavy, and it's an effort to keep my eyes open. I give in to the weight of my eyelids and allow my eyes to close. What's wrong with me? I feel like I've been dead for years and been forced back to life. My mouth is dry, as if someone packed it with sand. My breathing is deep. Light shines on my face; that's probably what woke me.

My eyes flutter open, and I look at the ceiling. It's unfamiliar. Without moving my head, I flash my eyes to the light. A beam of sunshine splits the curtains and illuminates the bed. Panic rises in my chest as I think of my last memory. Gabor was still in my apartment as I'd attempted to call Peter. He covered my mouth and held a gun to my head. He told me he was sorry and hated doing it, as he commanded me into a chair. He made me drink something and forced me out of the building and into his car.

As we drove, I felt my body grow heavy. I fought to stay awake but eventually gave in. Now I'm in a house I don't know on a bed I don't recognize. I sit up, and my mind spins. I collapse back, my head hitting the pillow. I hear the click of a door and sense someone has entered the room. I lean toward the window, press my elbow into the mattress, and sit up.

Gabor stands at the end of the bed, staring down at me.

"Good morning," he says.

I glare at him and attempt to turn away but feel something restrict me. I look down at my leg and find a handcuff around my ankle. The other side is connected beneath the bed.

He shrugs. "Sorry about that."

"Why are you doing this?"

Gabor doesn't answer. He steps to the small table near the door and pours a glass of water. He comes toward me, holding the water. I desperately want a drink.

"Are you thirsty?"

My eyes remain cold, but I nod.

He extends the cup to me, and I take it from him. I'm desperate to feel the wetness on my lips, but I hesitate. I peer at the cup, then back at him.

"I didn't do anything to the water. You can drink it."

I know I shouldn't, but my thirst is too great. I guzzle the contents in seconds. He comes forward and reaches for the glass. I throw it at his head. He ducks just in the nick of time, and the cup shatters against the wall, causing a picture frame to crash to the ground. Shards of glass cover the floor. Gabor looks at the smashed frame, then back at me. I expect him to lash out. I'm surprised to see nothing but calm. He sits on the bed outside my reach.

"I guess I should have given you a plastic cup."

"Is that supposed to be a joke? Are you expecting me to laugh?"

He sighs and shakes his head.

"Why am I here?"

"Believe me, I wish you weren't. I wanted to marry you, Zsuzsa. If you would have just said yes, we'd be on our honeymoon now."

"Yeah, and I'd be married to a trafficker."

"Oh, Zsuzsa. I'm not a trafficker."

"Oh, really? Then why are you holding me against my will? Why am I here?"

"I know you don't believe me, but I love you. But I don't have a choice."

He's studying the palms of his hands and won't look at me. Either he's a great actor, or he's sincere. But how could he be sincere?

"If you loved me, you wouldn't chain me up."

He turns and faces me. "Tell me where Peter is. Tell me where he's hiding the girls."

"What girls?"

He shakes his head, and I see anger flash in his eyes for the first time. "You know what girls. Don't play dumb."

"Gabor, I really don't. What are you talking about?"

"You expect me to believe that? You had Peter's number under your phone. You've seen him."

"Last I knew, he was in New York. I haven't seen him since I visited him in the jail."

He stands from the bed and walks to the door. "Suit yourself."

"Wait."

Gabor turns back.

"Just tell me why you're doing this."

"They just want the girls. Zsuzsa, tell me where they are."

"I don't know what you're talking about."

His voice goes cold. "Yes, you do."

"I don't."

He shakes his head and turns away. "Fine. Then they have no use for you."

"Then let me go."

He chuckles and turns the knob. "There's only one way you're leaving here. He's had enough of you."

Chapter Thirty-Three

Director Toth

Present

"Good to see you again, Director. I trust you're well?" The president's secretary walks toward me down the stairs. He extends his hand, then turns back to retrace his steps. "The president is available. His prior meeting ended early. Thanks for being prompt."

"Of course," I say, following a half step behind him as we ascend the stairs of the president's palace. When we reach the office, I stand back, allowing him to check with the president before I enter. He exits the office and tells me to go ahead. I nod and enter. I'm surprised to see the president isn't behind his desk. He's sitting in the cozy area at the back of the spacious office that looks more like a living room. It has couches, a coffee table, and two leather wingback chairs.

"József," he says, motioning with a wave. "Come over here. I thought this might be a bit more comfortable."

I nod and walk toward him.

He stands and extends his hand. We shake, and I wait for him to tell me where to sit. He motions to the couch opposite him, and I take my place.

"Thank you for coming to see me."

"My pleasure, sir."

I've wondered what he might say since receiving notice yesterday that the president would like to see me. He was friendly the last time I was here, but his demeanor quickly changed. This time, he appears as pleasant as the previous. Will it continue?

He leans back and puts his arm up on the back of the couch. This time, he has no folder in front of him—nothing to reference.

"József, I called you here for a couple of reasons. First, I wanted to give my condolences on the death of Rákosi Gyula. I know he was a loyal employee for many years. I'm sure you feel as I do. His presence will be missed. I hope the perpetrator of the heinous crime will be brought to justice."

"He will, sir. He's in custody and will be arraigned soon. He'll pay for what he did."

He nods. "I appreciate that. Secondly, I wanted to congratulate and thank you. You're a man of your word. I received a report on missing young women yesterday. The numbers are greatly improved. You said you'd handle it, and you did. As you can imagine, a man in my position gets told many things. Sometimes, they're true. Unfortunately, most times they aren't. This is one of the rare times I've been told something accurate."

"Thank you, sir."

"No, thank you, József." He raises his leg and rests his foot on his other knee. "There's something you asked me when last we met, and I gave you a blunt answer. Do you know what I'm referring to?"

"I think I do."

"I want you to ask me that question again."

We stare at each other for a beat before I say, "President, do I have your support?"

He looks me in the eye and nods. "Yes, you do, Director."

After leaving the president's palace, I go home rather than return to the office. I don't think I realized how much anxiety I was carrying as I traveled to meet him. Hearing him tell me I have his confidence both relieved and excited me. My plan is working.

Pulling through the gate, I'm surprised to see Eszter's red Saab in the driveway. She isn't typically home at this hour. I enter the house, and she calls out, believing I'm our daughter, Ildiko.

"It's me," I call.

"József?" She comes around the corner of the kitchen, a drink in her hand and concern in her eyes. "What's wrong?"

"Nothing. In fact, I have good news."

She comes closer, and I can smell the liquor on her breath. Her drinking has escalated again.

"I just came from a meeting with the president. He gave me a full vote of confidence. He says he's looking forward to many more years of my leadership as director."

She steps forward and throws her arms around me. Her drink splashes on my shoulder. I push down the annoyance, letting her bask in the news.

"That's wonderful. Oh, József, I'm so happy for you."

"Thank you. I have a few phone calls to make. I'll be in my office."

She releases me, and I can see the hurt in her eyes. She's never understood what I do for her—the responsibility I carry. I turn and head down the hall as she stumbles back to the kitchen, probably to refill her glass.

I close the door behind me and dial the number.

"What do you have for me?"

"We went to Gyula's house. Searched the whole thing. No mention of Lili or the girl from the internet café."

"Hmm...I've scanned his work computer and files. Nothing there either."

"Is it possible he didn't have them? Maybe he wasn't hiding them?"

"It's possible. But if not him..." Farkas! Szabo had told me he saw them meeting at Heroes' Square the night before I killed Gyula. Farkas has them. "Farkas."

"What about him?"

"He's got them."

"Are you sure?"

"No, but I think it's likely. There's only one other alternative. Speaking of, how's the bartender?"

"She hasn't said anything yet."

"Is it because she doesn't know? Or because the appropriate leverage hasn't been applied?"

"I'm not sure."

"Find out."

"Yes, sir. What do you want to do about Farkas?"

"Let's search his apartment and put a tail on him. See if he'll lead us to them. We can't afford to have another cop killed right now."

"Okay, I'm on it."

"Get the bartender to talk. Do whatever you must, and be careful. He might come looking for her."

"She'll talk."

"I do have some good news. The president gave me his full vote of confidence today. It looks like the plan to halt operations worked. In a couple weeks, we can restart. Are plans still moving forward in the new location?"

"They are. We'll be ready."

Chapter Thirty-Four

Detective Szabo

After hanging up my jacket and starting my computer, I sit at my desk and stare at my team. I'm the last one to arrive this morning. After talking with Peter, I went home, drank half a dozen beers, and watched TV on mute. Director Toth is the mole? I was so sure it was Farkas. In fact, I'm still not sure it isn't. Even if Toth is the mastermind, who's to say Farkas isn't working with him? Has Peter even thought about that? I'm still not over the shock of seeing him. I never thought he'd be back in Budapest. Can I really trust him?

"Knock, knock."

I was lost in my thoughts and didn't see her approach.

"What can I do for you, Detective?"

"Sir, I'm headed out to follow up on a lead. A mother of a missing girl wants to talk."

"Okay."

"I might not be back today."

That seems odd, but I tell her, "Fine," and dismiss her.

I stand and follow her out of the office. Katona looks up and smiles, and I nod. Farkas doesn't look at me. I walk toward the restroom but continue down the hall. I exit the office and descend the stairs until I reach the jail level. The two guards inside the bars stand as I approach.

"Good morning, Detective," says the small, thin one. I've only talked to him a handful of times, but he's always pleasant. He's from somewhere here in Budapest. I don't remember his name. Csaba, maybe?

"Good morning."

"How can I help you?"

"How long do you keep records of people visiting the jail?"

He turns and motions with his head. "See those binders? There's a different one for every year."

I look and see at least ten on the shelf. "I'm working a case and need to see if a certain prisoner had any visitors. December of last year. Can I have that binder?"

"I can show it to you. We aren't allowed to let anyone take it from here without written consent from Director Toth."

"Okay, that's fine. I'll look at it here."

The guard pulls one binder from the shelf in the small storage room and hands it to me. It's a thick three-ring binder, and I'm unsure how to do this. There isn't any furniture in the sterile corridor, nowhere for me to sit, or a table to rest the binder on.

"Do you want a chair?" the guard asks.

"That'd be great. Thanks."

He slides his chair through the open gate, and I sit on the opposite side and begin to flip through. It's in order, and I find the middle of December. I scan the names and signatures of each visitor. Nothing. No mention of Director Toth. To be sure, I check a week before and after Agoston, the club manager's incarceration. Nothing. Could Toth have removed it? He certainly has the power. Maybe Peter was wrong. Perhaps that's not what Kovacs saw in the log. I continue to flip the pages. The sheets are simple. There's a column for printed name, date and time in, date and time out, and signature. I feel my frustration rise. There's no mention of Toth.

I'm about to give the binder back when I decide to scan the names and signatures again. I see the date and time when Kovacs and Peter had visited Agoston. And that's when I see it, just above their names. The name listed doesn't match the signature. The person who must have given a false name forgot to sign the wrong name. Shock and excitement course through me. I close the binder, return it to him, and thank the guard.

I climb the stairs and exit the jail, but I leave the building instead of returning to my office. Scanning the sidewalks, I head down the street, the blood hot in my veins with excitement. I find a telephone booth and pull out my wallet. I hold up the small note with the phone number and dial. After a few rings, the voice answers.

"Hello."

"Peter?"

"Yes."

"It's Szabo."

The connection isn't good, and I strain to hear him. "Yes."

"I looked at the visitor log in the jail. It wasn't Toth's name Kovacs saw. It wasn't him who visited the club manager."

"Okay."

"It was Varga. Detective Varga is our mole."

"You're sure?"

"Yes. She signed the wrong name on the log. She gave a false name but signed with her own signature. She made a mistake."

"Where is she now?"

"She just left the office. She said she had to go talk to the mother of a missing girl."

Chapter Thirty-Five

Peter

Peter exits the bus and walks two blocks until he reaches the white Volkswagen van parked along the side of the road. He moves to wrap on the side door before opening it, but the smell of fresh cigarette smoke permeates the exterior. Peter smiles, knowing Tom is awake. He opens the sliding door and enters the back of the van.

"My dreams have come true. I've been hoping I'd get some company out here, and I wanted it to be you, rather than that hideous-looking woman inside the house over there."

Peter sits on the bench behind Tom and scans the house.

"I see you're still following your wife's advice."

"What? You don't think I'm being sincere?"

Peter looks at Tom, then turns his attention back to the house. "Any movement?"

"Nothing since they went inside."

"Just Gabor and Zsuzsa? Nobody else?"

"Not that I've seen."

Peter purses his lips and rubs his beard. He takes off his hat and places it on the seat beside him.

"What's the plan?'

"I'm not sure yet."

"What's he doing? Why does he have her?"

"Good question. It always seemed convenient, his timing. He shows up at her restaurant after she's seen in the jail talking to me. They haven't been in contact since they were kids, then suddenly, he's there with a story about being divorced and lonely. After finding evidence that he's been following her, I was sure he was connected. This only proves it. Well, I should say it likely proves it. There's always the other scenario."

"Which is?"

"He's some crazy, obsessive stalker. Maybe that's why I found all that stuff in his house. I hope it's not that. I don't think it is."

"Is he going to hurt her?"

Peter shakes his head. "I don't think so. He's likely a patsy. He's holding her because he's been told to. As long as nobody else goes in there, she's safe."

"So you aren't going in?"

"Not yet. There's more I need to understand before that happens."

"So now what?"

"We wait until someone else comes or something changes. I don't think it'll be long."

Tom reclines the seat and extinguishes his cigarette. "Well, at least I finally get to spend the night with you." He folds his arms and closes his eyes.

Peter chuckles and rolls his eyes.

Tom smiles but doesn't open his.

Hours later, Peter wakes to a buzzing in his jacket. He pulls out the phone, extends the antenna, and pushes the answer button. It's Detective Szabo. He tells Peter about going to jail and reviewing the guest lists. At the end of the call, he tells Peter what he already knows: Detective Varga is working with Toth. He also tells him Varga left the office and is following up on a "lead." Peter ends the call and replaces the phone in his jacket.

"You wanted a little action?" he says to Tom.

Tom gives him a strange look. "I was just kidding about being happy to spend the night with you. Don't get any ideas. We're just friends."

"Okay, you need some new material."

Tom laughs. "What do you want me to do?"

"Stay here. You might have a visitor or two. I'm headed to the house. Honk the horn if you see an ambush coming my way, then get out of here. If you see a slight, fit woman, it's Detective Varga; stay low and wait."

"Understood."

Peter exits the van and walks across the street. He continues around the block, then climbs along the cinderblock fence bordering two houses until dropping down into the backyard of the house Zsuzsa's in. He keeps low, not worrying too much about being seen. Gabor has all the curtains drawn on the windows. Peter should be fine if he doesn't make any noise. He looks around, hoping Gabor left the dog at home. That would significantly complicate things.

After finding a spot along the side of the house where he's out of sight from both the front entrance and the windows, he hunkers down and waits. Fifteen minutes later, he hears a car pull up. He pauses to listen to a beep of the horn, but nothing comes. He creeps along the cinderblock wall to the spot next to the gate and withdraws his gun. Keys rattle on the other side as someone fiddles with the locked gate and pulls it open. Detective Varga steps through the opening, and Peter holds the gun to her head, covering her mouth with his hand. She has grocery sacks in both arms.

"Nice of you to come, Detective. If you make any noise, I'll shoot you. I don't have any problems with killing a trafficker."

Varga doesn't fight him and allows him to walk her across the street to the van. When they approach, the back door opens, but it's not Tom who opens it. Tom remains behind the wheel. Peter pushes Detective Varga into the waiting arms of Detective Farkas. Farkas handcuffs her arms behind her back and forces her onto the seat. Tom pulls the grocery sacks to him and looks through them.

Peter sighs. "What are you doing?"

"I'm hungry," Tom replies.

Peter shakes his head and turns to Farkas. "Thanks for coming."

"I wouldn't miss it."

They sit on either side of Detective Varga. She looks at them and pleads her case. "Peter, Farkas, what's going on? Why are you doing this?" She turns to Farkas. "He killed Kovacs, and now you're working with him?"

Farkas smiles. "Actually, *you* killed Kovacs. It's a pretty risky move driving your car through the railing on the bridge. You're lucky you survived. Was that Toth's idea? Did you wonder if he also wanted you out of the way?"

She stares at him, then turns to Peter with an expression like, "Can you believe this guy?"

"It's over, Detective," Peter tells her. "We know you're our mole in the task force. We know you're working with the traffickers. We know all about you and Director Toth. It took me a long time to figure out he's your uncle. I suspected you for a while, but you're pretty cold. Killing your own niece in Újpest." Peter clicks his tongue. "Did she recognize you? Is that what happened? Is that why she had to die?"

Her expression turns sour, and she looks away from Peter. She stares out the windshield, her face impassive.

Peter knows getting information from her will be challenging. He looks past her and talks to Farkas. "You know what I can't figure? What was the plan when she was the bait in the club that night? The night we took David into custody. What if Kovacs had decided to let her be taken? What then? Were they just going to let her go eventually? Was she going to escape on her own? Surely, she was going to come back to the task force."

Varga turns to look at him. Against her better judgment, she speaks. "Kovacs was never going to do that."

Peter shrugs. "You're probably right. But why give up David like you did? No loyalty there, huh?"

"David was becoming a liability. He had to go."

"Yeah, makes sense. Was he squeezing you for more money?"

She looks back out the windshield. Tom turns around, smiles at her, and winks.

Peter says to Farkas, "Why don't you take her? I think she's tired of talking." Peter exits the van and walks along the sidewalk. He pulls out his mobile phone and dials Szabo. "I need your help. They've got Zsuzsa."

Chapter Thirty-Six

Director Toth

Past

I walk through the office door, and I'm greeted by the plump woman sitting behind the desk.

"Hello, József."

"Magda," I say, sitting at the desk across from her. As always, she's wearing a lot of makeup. She tries desperately to hide the wrinkles around her eyes and mouth, hoping to hold on to the youth that has long since escaped her.

"Here's the list of expenses for the month," she says, sliding the folder to me. "And here are the cash receipts, minus the expenses." She slides a large, overstuffed envelope to me. I look at it without opening it.

"Good month, huh?"

"Better and better ever since you started."

Magda and I have gone through this same ritual for the last year. She's right; every month has been better than the previous. But judging by the envelope on the desk, this month has been a record. I pick up the list and run my finger down each line. I stop at one in particular.

"What's this?"

"What do you mean?" Her voice says innocence, but her actions don't confirm her tone. She brushes back her hair and looks at me without blinking. When I had first started running the cathouses for the boss, I'd found a discrepancy in the cash. Magda was skimming money off the top, and nobody had ever caught it. When I asked her about it, she acted like she is now.

"Why are the transportation costs so high?"

"Our driver had a problem. He was bringing a shipment from Romania when he had a blowout. The truck flipped, and some of the products were damaged."

"How damaged?"

"Killed."

"Hmm…" I continue looking down the list. If that were true, I'd be seeing expenses that would match. The acquisition costs are still the same ratio as I would expect, and why isn't there any evidence we bought a new replacement truck? I look at the overflowing envelope of cash on the desk and pick it up. This also doesn't make sense. "Did the truck driver survive?"

"Yes."

"Where is he? I want to talk to him."

She shakes her head. "He's gone. He's picking up another shipment. He won't be back for a week."

I stand and turn for the door but keep my eyes trained on her lying face. "I'll be back one week from today. Same time. Make sure he's here. No excuses."

One week later, at the exact time, I enter the office. Magda sits behind the desk, playing with the pencil.

"Hello, József."

"Where's the driver?"

"He's outside in the truck. He said something about the oil."

I turn and leave the room, walk down the stairs, then out the front door. I circle the building and find the delivery truck. The hood is open, revealing the engine. A man stands over it, looking but not actively working.

"You're the driver?"

He turns and nods. "Yes, my name is Miklos." He extends his hand, and I take it. I turn it over and notice his hands are clean—no dirt under the nails.

"Sounds like you had a rough ordeal a week ago. I'm glad you came out of it. Looks like you didn't take any damage."

"No, I was lucky. Thank you, sir."

I nod and look at the truck. "Is this the new truck?"

"Yes, sir."

"So tell me about the accident."

He looks me in the eye, then looks away. "Well, I'm driving back from the Transylvania area. That's where my pickup was. I put the girls in the back."

I raise my hand and stop him. "Product. You put the product in the back."

He nods. "Sorry, yes, the product. I put them in the back and then started on my way here. Along the way, I had a tire blowout. I lost control of the truck, and it flipped on me."

I chew on my cheek and nod. "Where was this?"

"Just on the other side of the border, near Szeged."

"Magda said it was near Kecskemét."

He clears his throat and nods. "That's right, it was near Kecskemét. Sorry, it was wild. I hit my head pretty good, and I don't remember everything."

"Did you lose any of the product?"

He smiles. "Nope. All came through okay. Full delivery once I got this truck."

"Good job. Come join me in the office. I think you deserve a bonus."

I can see the excitement on his face as he walks beside me. We enter the building, climb the stairs, and enter the office. Magda is still behind the desk. I ask the driver to sit, and he takes the seat across from Magda so he's looking at her. I walk to the side of her desk and unhook the telephone cord.

"Magda, sounds like this man did a great job. I think he deserves a bonus, don't you?"

She keeps her eyes on me as I walk back behind him, holding the telephone cord.

"Yes," she says warily.

I put my hand on the man's shoulder, then wrap the phone cord around his neck and pull back. He fights me, grabbing me and kicking his feet. Before long, the fighting subsides as his head turns purple. I barely look at him, keeping my eyes fixed on her. She's gone white. When I'm sure he's dead, I release him and let his body slump to the floor. I sit in the chair across from her, the one he had occupied, and fix my tie.

"Care to change your story?"

She looks at me, her complexion ashen. She nods.

"What really happened?"

"I stole the money."

"Good. I told you before that if you did it again, I'd kill you. Now, I have to be a man of my word."

Tears run down her cheeks. "No...no, please."

I don't really want to kill her because of the hassle it would cause for me.

"I'm sorry, Magda. I'm a man of my word. You don't want to make a liar out of me, do you?"

She shakes her head and looks down, whispering, "Please...oh, please."

I scratch my cheek and rub my chin. "I'll give you one more chance. But I need something from you. Something that makes it worth keeping you alive." I know exactly what I want from her, but she doesn't know I know. One of the other whores in the house told me. She said Magda had a secret she was keeping from me. This little episode gives me the leverage to pry it from her. She looks up, and I stare at her. She gets control of her crying and watches me, understanding evident in her eyes.

"Go ahead, tell me."

"It's about your father."

"The mayor?"

She shakes her head. "No, your real father."

A surge of anger wells up in me at the mention of him. That traitor got what he deserved. "What about him?"

"I know who killed him. Who turned him in."

I shouldn't care, but I do. "Who?"

"Your boss, the minister of the interior. The man who owns this house. He knew your father. He knew he was speaking out against the communist leaders and turned him over to the State Protection Authority. He used your father to move up, and it helped him get the position he has now. He's the reason your father was taken and put to death."

"How do you know this?"

"Many important men come here. Some want to impress the girls. They brag and tell stories. At one time, I was one of those girls. Believe it or not, I was the most popular among the male visitors, including the minister."

I give her a cold look, then stand and lean over the desk. Her lower lip trembles as she looks back at me. "As a thank-you for me not killing you, you're going to make sure there's an extra ten thousand forint in this envelope next month. I'll consider it a personal gift. And Magda, if you ever steal from me again, I'll kill your entire family."

Chapter Thirty-Seven

Director Toth

Present

I pick up the phone on my desk and dial the number. After two rings, no answer. Hmm, that's interesting. I can't think of the last time she let my call go unanswered, no matter what time of day. After a minute and a half of rings, I hang up. I sit with my elbows on my desk, hands under my chin. Where is she?

I exit my office and walk down the hall to the trafficking task force bullpen. It's nearly empty, with only Detective Katona at his desk. I glance over and see Szabo is gone also.

"Are you looking for Szabo, Director?" Katona asks.

I turn and look at him. He's leaning back in his chair, a pen in his mouth. "Where is everyone?"

He shrugs. "Kinda weird. Varga went to Szabo's office, talked to him for a few minutes, then left. Szabo went down the hall for a while, then came back. In the meantime, Farkas stood up, and I thought he was going to the bathroom. He either fell in or left, because he hasn't returned. After Szabo got back, he got a call, then left. You just missed him. I guess there must be a party, and I'm not invited."

"Did you have a break in a case? Did something happen?"

"Not that I know of. Things have been pretty quiet lately. Seems like the trafficking has slowed down a lot."

I nod and look around the room. I walk over to Varga's desk. Nothing seems out of the ordinary. It looks like she meant to leave when she did. Why? Where was she going?

"Anything I can do for you, sir?"

I look up at him. "No. If any of them come back, have them come to my office."

"Sure."

I leave, walk back down the hall, nod to Erzsi, enter my office, and pick up the phone. After a couple of rings, a voice answers. "Hello?"

"Laci."

"József?"

"Where's your daughter?"

"You're asking me?"

"She left the office, and nobody's seen her. Has she called you?"

"No. I haven't talked to her in a few days. Is she in trouble?"

"I'm not sure. I don't think so. I'll find her."

I hang up and lean back in my chair, steepling my fingers. The last time I'd talked to her, I told her to make the bartender, Zsuzsa, talk. Did she go there? Did Farkas follow her? Did he tell Szabo? Suddenly, I feel a flash of irritation. The bartender's my bargaining chip. If I lose her, I lose leverage. I stand and walk out of my office, pulling open the door.

Erzsi jumps as I step in front of her.

"I need you to do two things immediately."

She picks up a pen and notepad.

"Number one, we have a rogue agent. Evidence has come to light that Detective Farkas of the trafficking task force was involved in the murder of Rákosi Gyula and the reporter Béla. I need you to issue a warrant for his capture. It appears Detective Szabo is also involved. Both men are armed and dangerous. Deadly force is to be used in their capture if necessary."

Her eyes widen as she looks up at me, then focuses back on the task.

"Second, I need a SWAT team dispatched to this address." I hand her a sticky note with the house address written on it. "I'm heading there now. Have them meet me there as soon as possible."

I don't wait for a response and walk down the hall.

Katona is still sitting at his desk. He jumps and nearly falls from his chair when I speak to him. "Katona, come with me."

Chapter Thirty-Eight

Detective Szabo

I almost missed it. I nearly drove right past. All the roads look the same in this little town of Érd. Peter told me the street name is Bogdánfy. Luckily, nobody is behind me, and I can throw it in reverse. Small houses line either side, and I search for 1117. I'm only four houses away. I park on the side of the road, but before I can exit the car, Peter's standing beside me.

"It's that house on the right," Peter says. "She's in there with her boyfriend, Gabor."

"Boyfriend? When did she get a boyfriend? I thought that was you?"

Peter gives me a sardonic look. "A lot changed while I was gone."

"So, if he's her boyfriend, why is he doing this?"

"He works for Toth." Peter considers telling him about Varga but decides that information can wait. He doesn't want any more questions right now.

"How do you want to do this?" Szabo asks.

"You go in the front; I'll go in the back. It's only him and Zsuzsa. Don't shoot unless you must, and make sure it's him, not her."

Szabo nods.

"Give me five minutes, then come in the front gate. I'll motion to you. Once I'm in the back, go in."

Peter walks down the street. I look at my watch, then lean against the cinderblock wall. Zsuzsa has a boyfriend? Why didn't she tell me? Then again, what business is it of mine? Still...I've seen her several times since Peter left. I've never been her type, but that doesn't stop my hope. Maybe that shows she doesn't care for Peter like I thought. I look back down at my watch. It's been five minutes.

I creep along the wall, reach the gate, and move it open. It creaks, and I inwardly groan. I look at the house. The curtains are drawn, and nobody seems to be watching. I enter the yard and look around—Peter's on the side of the house. He holds up ten fingers and mouths "seconds." I nod, and he's gone. I creep forward up the stairs, silently counting. When I reach ten, I withdraw my gun and try the door. To my surprise, it opens. The room's small. Not much more than two hundred square feet. There's a couch and a couple chairs. A TV's on, but nobody's watching it. Where is he?

I enter the room and close the door behind me. I look around the corner and see the back of the house. There's a small kitchen with a table and counter. Peter holds a finger to his lips. I nod and follow him as he enters the hallway. There are three doors, two on the right and one on the left. Peter and I line up on either side of the door, and he motions to me. I nod, and he opens the door. I come around the corner, gun up, but it's an empty bathroom. I check the tub and the closet—nothing.

A muffled cry comes from the room further down the hall. We line up on either side of the door like before, and Peter motions to me. He opens the door, and I enter with my gun forward. I stop short when I see Zsuzsa being held by a man, a gun pressed to her temple.

"Put down the gun," the handsome man says.

I hold up my hands, then slowly bring them down, keeping my eyes on him. His eyes are trained on me. I glance behind me. Peter's gone. What a coward.

"Put these on." The man holds up a pair of handcuffs and throws them at me.

I intentionally fumble the catch to look back as I pick them up off the floor. Where did Peter go?

The man tells me to sit on the bed when the handcuffs are secured. He pushes Zsuzsa down next to me. He keeps the gun trained on us.

"Are you okay?" I ask her.

"Shut up!" he says, aiming his gun at my head. "You only talk when I ask you a question. Who are you?"

"Me?"

"Yeah, you, fatso. Who are you?"

I glare at him and imagine smashing his pretty little face. "Your worst enemy."

He chuckles. "Are you alone, tough guy?"

"Do you see anyone else here?"

"Why'd you come? Where's Varga? What did you do with her?"

I can't help the surprise that registers on my face. Before I can answer, a gun appears and is held to the man's head. Peter stands beside him. "Give me the gun."

"Peter," Zsuzsa whispers.

I turn and look at her and can see the admiration in her eyes.

"Szabo," Peter says. "Get your gun. I'll keep mine on Gabor."

I stand from the bed and retrieve my gun from the floor. I hold it in my handcuffed hands and turn it toward Gabor.

"Keep your gun on him."

"Put your hands over your head and sit on the ground," I command.

"Where are the keys to the cuffs?" Peter asks.

"In a drawer in the kitchen."

Peter turns to me. "Watch him."

I nod, and he leaves the room. I look over at Zsuzsa. She's tousled, and her hair is a mess, but I don't think she's ever looked better. Peter returns and goes to her. They lock eyes. I'd be blind not to see the chemistry between them.

"Are you okay?" Peter whispers.

She nods, and he reaches for the shackle on her ankle. He releases her, then comes over to me. He positions his body so he can see Gabor while unlocking my handcuffs. When my hands are free, he walks closer to Gabor, holding his gun. "This is quite a way to show a girl you love her."

Gabor looks up at him. "At least I didn't leave the country without telling her."

Peter ignores the jab. "Why'd you do this? Toth told you to?"

Gabor shakes his head.

"Look, Toth is going down. It's just a matter of days. You can help yourself by talking to us or burn with him and Varga. It's your choice."

"No, it's *your* choice. Toth's on his way here, and he's not alone."

I hear a car door and go to the window. A black Audi just pulled up outside. Toth and Katona get out of the car.

"Peter, he's here. Katona's with him. They're watching for someone else. I think they have more coming."

I look at Zsuzsa. She can't be here. We've got to get her out.

Peter joins me at the window. "Take Zsuzsa. Get her out of here."

As much as I would love that, I know it's not me she wants. I'll never mean anything to her. She might not ever care for me, but I can do something for her now.

"No. You know the back way. Take her. Get her out. I'll stay here with Gabor. I'll hold them off so you can get away."

Peter, knowing what I'm suggesting, shakes his head. I push him toward the door.

"Get out of here. Take Zsuzsa. I'll be fine."

We stare at each other, and finally, he nods and extends his hand to Zsuzsa. As she passes me, she brushes her hand over my arm.

"Thank you," she says.

I gaze at her, and my heart hurts for what I want so badly but will never have. How can I tell her what's in my heart? Does she know that her simple touch makes it all worth it? The feel of her hand brushing my arm and the gratitude I see in her eyes is all I need.

She gives her hand to Peter, and as they leave the room, she looks back at me again. I smile, and she smiles back. I'd do anything for her, including giving my life.

I pick up the handcuffs and throw them to Gabor when they're out of sight.

"Your turn to put these on."

Once he has them secured, I return to the road. A SWAT van pulls up, and multiple officers stream out. I've got to buy Peter and Zsuzsa time to escape. I grab Gabor by the arm and pull him up. We walk into the front room. I part the window curtain. Toth must have twenty officers, and they're lined up on the street receiving final instructions. I grab Gabor and throw open the door with my gun pressed to his head. I've got to give Peter and Zsuzsa as much time as possible. Gabor knows too much. I can't let him talk.

Chapter Thirty-Nine

Zsuzsa

Peter holds my hand as we walk down the hall. When we reach the kitchen, he releases me and looks out the back window. After looking around, his gaze returns to me.

"Stay close. Keep low and out of sight. We're going to go to the back wall. I'll help you up. Drop into the neighbor's yard, and move away from the house."

I nod, and he opens the back door. He steps out, and I'm behind him, blinking against the harsh sun. I've been in the house for a day now with little natural light. After a few seconds, my eyes adjust as I run beside him.

He gives me a boost when we reach the fence. I crawl along the top of the wall and drop down to the yard below. Almost immediately, Peter joins me. He puts his finger to his lips and points to the front of the house. We run beside the wall when I hear a gunshot. I'm tempted to look back, but Peter keeps running.

Once we're in the front of the house, he boosts me over the front gate, and I drop down. I look at him through the gate. He points to the left and whispers, "Run." I bolt down the street. When I reach the street's end, he's beside me. He grabs my hand and pulls me with him. We continue to run away from the gunshots popping behind us. After probably ten minutes, which feels much longer, my lungs are burning. My legs feel like lead. Even though he's older than me, I'm impressed with his condition. He seems unfazed. He looks at me, and I know he sees my exhaustion. We run one more block and reach a small shopping center.

Peter stops running and takes my hand. As we walk, he pulls a mobile phone from his jacket and dials a number.

"Where are you?" he says into the phone.

Someone on the other end speaks, but I can't hear what is said.

"We're by the Spar. Come get us. We'll be hiding behind it."

When we reach the end of the building, he pulls me back behind it.

Once I've caught my breath enough to talk, I say, "Who was that?"

"A friend. Stay here."

He walks around the corner and disappears. Unsure what to do, I stay put. Two minutes later, he's back.

"Looks like we're okay for now. But I'm sure Toth has already issued warrants for us. We'll be hunted by every cop in Hungary within minutes."

He looks at me, and I have so many things I want to say to him. But none of those things matter right now. I say the only thing that does: "Thank you."

He smiles. "You're welcome. But it's Szabo you should be thanking. He's still there."

"What's going to happen to him?"

He shakes his head. "I'm not sure."

"How did you know?"

"Know what?"

"That Gabor had me. How did you know I was there?"

Before he can answer, a white van pulls up with an old man behind the wheel. Peter takes my hand and opens the back door. He lets me go first, then follows me in, sitting beside me. He slams the door shut while the old guy pulls out.

"Took you long enough," Peter says.

"Watch it. I would have left you. You're just lucky you had her."

Peter smiles. "You know where you're going?"

"I'm not that old." He looks in the rearview mirror at me, then back to Peter. "Aren't you going to introduce us?"

"Zsuzsa, this is Tamás. Tamás, this is Zsuzsa."

"It's a pleasure to meet you, Tamás."

He actually turns in his seat to look at me, no longer watching the road. "Zsuzsa, believe me, the pleasure is all mine."

Chapter Forty

Director Toth

Present

Finally, we reach the house. I've never driven faster. After getting in the car, Katona began asking questions. Where are we going, was his first. My answer was short and blunt. He didn't catch on. His second, where is the rest of the team, was all I could take. This time, I stared at him, not speaking. He caught on, and his cheeks flushed. From that point, he kept his mouth shut, looking out the window and watching me drive.

After parking in front of the house, I shut off the car. A woman across the street is watering her plants on her front porch. I show my badge and instruct her to go inside. She drops her watering pail and nearly flies into the house. I turn around and look back the way we came. I should hear sirens by now, but I don't. Wait...is that something in the distance? It's faint, but it's getting louder. I turn to Katona, "Two members of your team are moles for the trafficking syndicate in Budapest, Szabo and Farkas. Detective Varga learned of their actions and informed me. They've taken her hostage with another woman and man in this house."

Katona's mouth drops open, and he stares at me wide-eyed.

"SWAT is on the way. We'll assess the situation, then take the house by force, if necessary."

He nods as the SWAT vehicle pulls up, along with several police cars.

The SWAT commander, Captain Racz, exits the vehicle and approaches. He's tall, over six feet. Although he's late forties, he looks like he could crush twenty-year-olds in a fitness competition. "Sir, what do we have?"

"Detectives Szabo and Farkas are working with a human trafficking syndicate in the city. Detective Varga found them out, and they're holding her hostage in the house, along with two others, a male and female." I pass him photos of Varga, Farkas, and Szabo. "They're armed, trained, and dangerous."

"Understood, sir."

Movement at the front of the house catches my eye. Gabor is standing on the porch with Szabo behind him. Szabo is shielding himself with Gabor's body. He holds a gun to Gabor's head.

"I have more hostages inside," Szabo shouts. "If anyone tries to enter, I'll start killing them. Starting with him."

The captain looks at me.

"You have full autonomy on this mission, Captain. I want the women alive. Do what you have to with Szabo and Farkas."

He nods and calls out instructions to his officers. Katona and I stand by the black Audi and watch officers surround the house. Captain Racz walks to the front gate and calls out to Szabo. "Let them go, Szabo. We can talk about this. No need to hurt anyone. Let's work together to make sure everyone lives, including you."

"I won't come out until Director Toth pays for what he's done."

"What has he done?"

"You won't believe it if I tell you."

"I'll hear you out. I promise. But I need you to do something for me. I need you to release a hostage. Let one of the women go. That'll show me who you are. Show me you're a good guy, and you've been mistreated."

Szabo remains silent. His body and face are obscured by shadow. "I can't do that."

"Szabo, you have to work with me. I can't help you unless you help me."

Szabo pulls Gabor back into the house. A dog barks from a few houses down, but other than that, there isn't a sound.

"What's he doing?" Katona asks me.

"I'm not sure."

The captain looks at me, and I stare back at him. He waits several seconds, then shouts, "Szabo, I need proof of life. I need to see the women. Show me you haven't hurt them."

No response.

"Szabo," the captain shouts. "You have three minutes. If I don't have proof of life, we're coming in." The captain sets a timer on his watch and instructs his officers outside the house.

He shouts to Szabo when the time reaches two minutes, then one minute.

At thirty seconds, he calls, "Szabo, you have twenty seconds. Don't do this. Show me proof of life."

The front door swings back open, but it's empty. Nobody is visible.

"Director Toth isn't who he says he is. He's the leader of the human trafficking syndicate in Budapest. Detective Varga is working with him. They should be the ones you're arresting."

"That's not going to work, Szabo. You know better than that."

Silence inside the house.

"Okay, I'm coming out. Don't shoot."

Gabor is visible again in the doorframe, with Szabo right behind. Szabo's gun is still held to the side of Gabor's head.

"We're coming out. Don't shoot."

Szabo walks Gabor down the stairs, still holding the gun to his head. Once they reach the bottom, they take three steps toward the captain, then stop.

"Szabo, put the gun down," the captain commands.

Guns are aimed at Szabo from all around the house.

In a softer, gentler voice, the captain repeats his demand.

Szabo looks at him, then looks past the gate at me. He says nothing, only mouths the words, "You did this."

He pulls the trigger, and blood sprays from Gabor's head as he falls to the ground.

The many guns aimed at Szabo open fire. He takes shots to the head, back, chest, and legs. An instant later, he lies on the ground, riddled with bullet holes.

Dead.

Chapter Forty-One

Peter

Peter feels a buzzing in his jacket pocket. He removes the mobile phone, extends the antenna, and pushes the answer button. He expects to hear the voice of Farkas on the other end. Instead, it's female.

"Peter?"

"Yes?"

"It's Renata."

"What's wrong?"

"They found me."

Peter grips the phone tighter. "Who found you? Where are you?"

"I'm at Dominic's. The traffickers. They found me. They've been asking about me at my school. I didn't know what to do. I came to Dominic's, and he had your number."

"Where is Dominic's? Where are you in the city?"

"I'm in the Belváros in Pest."

"Can you get to Moszkva Tér?"

"Yes, I think so."

Peter looks out the windshield of the van. He sees a sign indicating they're only five kilometers from Budaörs.

"I'll be there as quick as I can. Wait for me in the square outside the subway station. Go now. Stay out of sight."

Renata says she will and hangs up. Peter puts the phone back in his jacket.

"Moszkva?" Tom asks.

"Yep."

Twenty minutes later, they pull up at Moszkva Tér. Peter scans the square but doesn't see Renata. He looks at Zsuzsa, who's asleep on the bench behind them.

"Stay here," Peter tells Tom. "I'll go look for her."

Peter climbs out of the van and walks through the square, scanning the people. When he reaches the center near the subway station, he looks around. Two girls stand in the shadows near a large tree but look nothing like Renata. He continues to scan the crowd when he feels a tap on his shoulder. He turns around to see the girls standing in front of him.

"Peter," the girl who tapped him says.

He stares at her, amazed by the transformation. The girl is covered in black, other than the jean skirt. Even her hair is jet black. She wears thick black makeup to complete the ensemble and has multiple piercings.

"Renata?"

She nods. "This is my friend, Zoe."

Peter smiles at the other girl. She looks more like what Peter had expected from Renata. "Come on. Let's go."

Peter leads the way, and once they reach the van, he opens the back door for them. Zsuzsa's awake now and sits on the opposite side of the bench seat.

"This is Zsuzsa," Peter says to the girls. "The old man up there is Tamás."

Zsuzsa extends her hand to both of them while they sit on the seat beside her, and Peter slams the door. After Peter climbs in beside Tom, Tom looks at him.

"Old man, really?"

"What? You aren't old?"

"You don't have to remind me and point it out to everyone we meet."

Peter smiles. "You're right. I don't have to... By the way, you must be tired by now. Why don't you let me drive."

He and Tom switch seats while Zsuzsa and the girls get acquainted. Before long, they seem to be fast friends. Zsuzsa and Renata share their stories about being abducted at the club and taken to Ukraine. Zoe interrupts with a question here and there, and Peter and Tom are content to listen to the women converse.

After an hour's drive, Peter pulls up to the house in Tatabánya. He turns to Tom once he's parked the van. "How's your sister going to feel about more guests?"

"Lousy." Tom grunts. "But then I'll remind her what these girls have been through. All she has to do is hear their stories, and she'll be anxious to help." He looks back at the women and then says in a whisper, "How long will they be here?"

Peter shakes his head. "I'm not sure."

He nods and opens his door, then opens the back door for the women. They climb out, and Peter goes to Zsuzsa.

"Are you okay?"

"I'm fine. I wouldn't mind something to eat, though."

"Let's see what we can do."

Tom walks up to the front door and knocks. After a few seconds, his younger sister answers.

"Miss me?"

She looks at him, then at the four others behind him.

"Room for a few more?" he says with a grin.

She opens the door wider but gives him a look.

"Come in. We're just having dinner. I'll see if I can make it stretch."

She shows them into the kitchen where Lili, Farkas, and Julia, the internet-café girl, sit eating. When they see the four of them, they stand. Peter greets them all and introduces those who haven't met. Tom's sister uses every bowl she has to feed the group, but Farkas must have warned her more would be coming. She has plenty of food. Peter is famished and badly wants to eat the paprikás krumpli in the bowl before him, but a thought strikes.

Peter turns to Farkas. "Where's Varga?"

Farkas points to the other side of the room. Varga sits on the ground, her hands bound behind her back. Her ankles are tied with rope. Duct tape covers her mouth.

"She wouldn't shut up. I finally had to bring out the tape."

Peter smiles.

"Don't worry. We'll feed her. I just thought we'd go first."

After fifteen minutes of little conversation and lots of chewing and smacking of lips, the group slows their eating. Peter feels he could eat everything in the house but decides to slow down, too. He notices Farkas look at Lili, then whispers to Peter, "Can we talk for a minute?"

"Sure."

Farkas motions with his head, and Peter and Lili follow into the other room. Once they're alone, Farkas closes the door.

"Go ahead and show him," Farkas says to Lili.

Peter turns and looks at her.

"You know how you asked me to figure out a way to interview each of the trafficking victims to help expose Toth?"

"Yes."

"Well...I may not work for Duna Television anymore, but I can still interview them, and we can still get it broadcast."

"Video?"

"Exactly."

Lili picks up the remote control on the table and presses play. On the screen, she's sitting with Julia in this very room.

"Will you tell me your name?" Lili asks.

Julia nods. "My name is Horváth Julia."

"And Julia, where do you work?"

"I work at the internet café near Váci Utca."

"How do you know Toth József, the director of the Hungarian National Police?"

"Well, I don't know him. Or, at least, I didn't until recently. He came into the café a couple times."

Lili holds up a photo of Director Toth and shows it to the camera and Julia. "Is this the man you saw?"

"Yes."

"Tell us what happened after that."

"One day, I was leaving work after my shift. As I walked home, a man stopped me. He showed me his badge and told me his name was Detective Farkas. The detective told me my life was in danger. He explained that several emails had been traced to our café and were sent by a murderer. The murderer tried to cover his tracks and would be coming for me. He then showed me that picture."

"This one of Director Toth?"

"Yes."

"And you recognized him?"

"Yes."

"What happened then?"

"I told Farkas that Director Toth was in the café. That he only stayed for a few minutes and then would leave. He always kept to himself."

"Julia, thank you for telling us your story."

Lili stops the tape and turns back to Peter. "We can do this with each woman. Like witnesses in a court of law. Testimony after testimony against Director Toth."

Peter smiles. "Perfect. This is exactly what I was hoping for."

Chapter Forty-Two

Director Toth

Past

The minister's dead body lays before me. I've been planning to kill him for months, and tonight, all my planning finally came to fruition. Killing someone of his standing isn't easy. It takes work. Significant work. He's always got someone around. Someone he's meeting with or talking to. He's an important man with many responsibilities.

When planning his death, I knew one thing was nonnegotiable: there would never be a body. I've long believed the perfect murder includes no evidence. What larger piece of evidence is there than the body? No body means no confirmation of death. Which means he could still be alive, as far as anyone knows.

Once I knew that, I worked on the next part of the plan. I wondered how I would make it look like the minister had left. And why would he go? Those were questions I noodled on for weeks when it suddenly hit me. Corruption. It's not a stretch; he is corrupt. As corrupt as anyone could be. But how would I plant evidence of his evil-doing without it getting back to me? How could I keep the trafficking alive without investigations? And even then, how could I put this plan in place without the minister knowing?

For weeks, I considered different options when it finally hit me. I'd do precisely what he did to my father. I'd plant evidence that he was an anti-communist. That he actually hated the party and wanted out. He had turned traitor on those who had helped him get where he was. Their hate for him would be catastrophic. He'd have to run to save his life.

Once I developed my story, it became easy to frame. I wrote letters on his letterhead to anticommunist groups. I made them believe he was with them. He was working the backchannels of the government supporting their cause. I gave them hope. The irony is the minister would be the last person to support them. No bigger communist existed. Karl Marx would envy his passion. Communism had made him rich beyond measure.

Nobody, except for me, knew just how wealthy the minister was. The cathouses were just a part of it. He was selling women all around the world. He'd abduct them in Czechoslovakia, Ukraine, Romania, Serbia, and Yugoslavia, then bring them to Budapest. Using his power as minister, he'd invite wealthy men to come to Budapest and bid on them. The girls would be shipped off to the highest bidder, with nobody knowing where they came from.

For a year and a half, I've been the face of his empire. I have connections with other countries, both in acquisition and buying. I know where he keeps his money. I know everything. Now it's mine.

When I considered what to do with the body, a question repeated in my head. Where is the least surprising place to find a dead body? A graveyard, of course. Nobody questions a dead body in a graveyard. Graveyards are hallowed ground. People come to graveyards to honor the dead. For years, a dead body lays in the earth undisturbed.

Sweat glistens on my forehead as I complete the dig. It's deep enough now. I grab the minster and drop him in the hole with a thud. I push a mound of dirt on top of him. It's a giant pile that took me two hours to complete. It takes only fifteen minutes to bury him and erase any evidence. I walk to the car, get in, and drive away. Tomorrow, I'll empty his accounts, pay off the customs agents, and reveal the evidence of his defection from the communist party. Tomorrow I'll be the minister in everything but title.

Chapter Forty-Three

Director Toth

Present

Five ties hang on the rack behind my office door: blue, red, and black. I select one of the red ties and step to the mirror. My wife tells me red demonstrates power and dominance. That's what I want. I want Farkas, wherever he is, to feel fear when he looks at me. My message will be clear and direct.

I stride out of my office and down the stairs toward the podium in the Hungarian National Police Headquarters. At least thirty reporters, camera crew, and administrative staff sit waiting. Molnar Ferenc, my wife's sister's son, stands at the bottom of the stairs, waiting.

"Uncle, the podium is all set for you. The press has been informed that you will address today's events and answer questions. As always, I'm here if you need me."

I nod and pat him on the shoulder as I pass. I prefer him to call me Uncle instead of Director. I stride to the podium, adjust the microphone, and a hush falls over the crowd.

"Today, at one thirty p.m., there was an incident in Érd. Following a tip, SWAT was dispatched to a house along Bogdánfy Utca. A gunman held four people hostage inside the home. When officers arrived, they attempted to negotiate with the instigator of the standoff. The suspect opened fire on the officers after killing two of the hostages. Both deceased hostages were male, including Detective Szabo of the National Police and Borsos Gabor of Budapest. The gunmen fled the scene with two female hostages. A national search is underway to find the perpetrator of this and other crimes. His name is Farkas László, a former member of the Hungarian National Police. A photo of Mr. Farkas is being distributed to each of you now. He's considered armed and very dangerous. A tip line has been created for those to call if they have any information about the hostages or Mr. Farkas. Checkpoints have been established on all highways and freeways in and out of Budapest. They will remain in place until Mr. Farkas is found and the hostages are returned safely. I'll now take questions."

Every member of the press jumps to their feet. I point to the woman in the front row with the navy suit and pen in her hand. "Director, can you tell us what caused the standoff today? And should people be worried more of the same could take place near them?"

"I can't give any other details about the case at this time. It's still an ongoing investigation; however, I will offer this piece of advice to Mr. Farkas. Turn yourself in now. Don't make this worse for you or your family."

"Sir, does that mean Mr. Farkas has a wife and kids?"

"No. But he does have parents and siblings who love him. He should turn himself in to prevent any further suffering on their part."

It's as clear as I can speak to him. I trust he got the message—turn yourself in, or your family will suffer. Shouts of "Director" emanate from the crowd, and I point to a man standing near the back.

"Sir, any idea why Detective Szabo was there?"

"Detective Szabo was chasing a lead, which led him to Mr. Farkas. We believe Mr. Farkas was involved in other murders as well."

"Can you tell us who?"

"The reporter, Halasz Béla, and the woman he was found with."

A collective gasp goes up around the room.

"As I said before, he's an extremely dangerous man, and if you see him, get distance immediately and call the tip line. Thank you."

I walk away from the podium as reporters continue to hurl questions. I hear my phone ringing once I'm back upstairs and in my office.

"Hello?"

"József, what's going on? What's the latest?"

It's President Madl. "Sir, I just held a press conference and explained that Detective Farkas is the suspect at large. It would appear he's also the head of the trafficking syndicate in the country. Detectives Szabo and Varga tracked him to the house in Érd. When they confronted him, he killed Szabo and took Varga as a hostage. We've set up roadblocks around the city. We'll find him."

"Keep me informed."

"I will."

I hang up, then the phone rings again.

"Hello?"

"József?"

"Laci."

"Where's my daughter?"

I've been expecting this call. "Farkas has her. She's a fantastic agent. She'll be okay until we find her."

"Why did he take her?"

"It's hard to know. But it looks like he was involved in the trafficking in the country. Your daughter discovered his guilt."

Silence on the other end of the line.

"Laci, she'll be okay. He needs her alive as collateral. She'll get through this."

"Find her, József. I'm counting on you."

"I will."

I hang up and rest my elbows on the desk while covering my eyes. A thought keeps rattling around my head: where did he go, and who's helping him?

Chapter Forty-Four

Director Toth

Past

I sit in my office reviewing paperwork when I hear a commotion in the hallway. I stand from my desk, open the door, and look out. Several people are congregating around the TV in the small kitchen area. I look to my right and see my secretary is gone. Odd. I walk down the hall, and several agents see me.

"Sir, have you heard the news?"

I shake my head, and he points to the TV.

"The wall is coming down in Berlin. Germany is going to be reunited."

I frown and step closer to the television. The news anchor confirms what he'd just said. Images flash on the screen of people climbing on the wall and joining the other side.

Someone asks the very thing that's rattling around my head: "Sir, what does that mean for us? Will anything change here?"

I shake my head, my eyes still glued to the TV. "I don't know."

We all watch for ten minutes until they replay the broadcast.

I turn to my employees. "Get back to work. Nothing has changed for us. We'll let you know if it does."

I walk back to my office as the group scatters. I close the door and pick up the phone. I dial the minister.

"I don't know anything yet, József."

"It's true then."

"Yes. I'm not sure what else will change. But some are speculating the entire Soviet Union will collapse. The Russians may be pulling out of Hungary soon. I'll let you know more when I know."

I hang up and lean back in my chair, the paperwork forgotten. I'm a communist. I've belonged to the party my whole adult life. Will the government of the country change? How will that affect me? Not just here but with my business pursuits. My cathouses and trafficking have never been stronger. Business is booming, and my Suisse bank account continues to grow. Will the government be reformed? Will I lose my position and influence?

As I ponder the implications of today's news, I make a resolution. Whatever happens, whatever political change may be in store, I'm going to find a way to continue my operations. I'll do whatever is necessary, whether it be bribe or kill. I'll end up on top.

Chapter Forty-Five

Zsuzsa

I don't remember the last time I slept on the floor. Maybe when I was fourteen, when I'd had a sleepover with Gabor's sister, but I didn't feel then like I do now. There just aren't enough beds in this house. I tried to sleep on a chair, but that didn't work. Finally, I took my blanket and lay on the rug in the kitchen. Renata and Zoe took one of the beds, Lili took a couch, and Julia took the other. Peter and Tom had a bench each in the van, and Farkas slept in a chair. Tom's sister, Reka, is sweet to allow us to take over her house. I hope there aren't more nights like this.

During breakfast, Lili explained the plan to all of us. She asked us to speak about Director Toth on camera. She'd ask the questions; all we had to do was answer. I was happy to do it. Everyone seemed willing, except for Renata. She was hesitant, and who can blame her? But, after Zoe spent some time encouraging her, she agreed. Lili said she had already interviewed Julia, and it went well. Julia agreed, saying it was pretty easy.

After breakfast was cleared, Peter helped Lili set up the camera while the rest of us made ourselves presentable. The plan was for Detective Farkas to go first, then me, and finally Renata. I asked Lili why not all of us simultaneously, and she said it would be more difficult with the camera setup. She also wanted to treat it like a lawyer questioning a witness in a courtroom. Once everything was set, Detective Farkas went in with Lili while Tom and Reka watched. Peter ran the camera. There wasn't enough room for all of us, so Renata, Zoe, and I sat in the kitchen.

I can see Renata's anxiety as we sit at the kitchen table. Her leg bounces up and down, and she alternates between looking at her hands and staring out the window, barely aware of my conversation with Zoe. At one point, Zoe says something about school and then lightly pushes Renata's shoulder, looking for confirmation.

"Do you know that I was in Ukraine at the same time as you?" I say to Renata.

She doesn't hear me.

"Hey, earth to Renata," Zoe says, waving a hand before her eyes.

She blinks a couple of times and looks at us.

I smile and repeat myself.

"You were? In the room?"

"No, they didn't take me for the same reason they took you. I was in the club trying to find out information about the trafficking. They abducted me, thinking I was a threat. I was held in a warehouse. Peter and Detective Kovacs saved me. They also saved the other girls who had been held with you."

"Really?"

"Yep. I know you feel guilty for leaving them behind, but you shouldn't. You did the right thing to get out. Your actions saved those girls. If you hadn't escaped and called Peter, he wouldn't have known to come to Ukraine. You saved those girls, and you saved me."

Tears well up in her eyes as she looks at me.

"Thank you, Renata. Thank you for saving me."

A tear rolls down her cheek.

"And do you know what else?"

"What?"

"Agnes isn't your fault either. It's Director Toth's fault. He's the person behind this, and we have a chance to stop him. It won't bring Agnes back, but it will save other girls like her in the future. Women like you and me won't be abducted by him."

The door opens, and Farkas comes out of the room. He looks at me. "You're up, Zsuzsa."

I nod and stand, but Renata grabs my hand before I can take a step.

"Zsuzsa, would it be okay if I go first? If I don't go now, I might chicken out."

I look in her eyes and can't help feeling proud of her. She's been through so much at such a young age.

"Of course. Go right ahead." I give her a hug and whisper in her ear, "You're such a strong girl."

She asks Zoe to go with her, and I sit back at the table. I expect Farkas to come over, but he doesn't. Instead, he walks back into the room. After a few seconds, Peter exits and shuts the door. He comes and sits at the table across from me.

"I hope you don't mind me sitting with you for a minute."

"Of course not."

He smiles at me. "Farkas is probably better with the camera than me anyway. Technology has never been my thing."

We smile at each other, and I wonder what's going through his mind.

"Zsuzsa..." He pauses. "I'm sorry I left Hungary without telling you. I'm sorry I got you caught up in all this."

I shake my head. "Peter, you've already apologized for leaving. I forgive you. And as far as getting me in this mess, if you remember right, I was already in it. I worked for Andras."

"I know. But you got taken in the club, then Gabor took you."

"I volunteered in the club, and Gabor came to the restaurant because I was trying to talk to the woman in Újpest. Stop giving yourself all the credit. You aren't as important as you think you are."

He chuckles. "Okay."

We sit smiling at each other again.

"We never got to go on our date. When this is all over, how about we try again?"

I've got to give him credit; I didn't think he'd ask. But I can't, and I've got to be honest with him. "Peter, I care about you. I'll be forever grateful. You've saved me at least three times, and I'd be dead without you. I care about you so much. But I think we'd be better off as friends."

His face falls, and I can see the disappointment in his eyes.

I rush on, feeling the need to explain. "After what happened with Gabor, I need time for myself. And you lost your wife only, what, a year ago? Things just haven't been right for us. Maybe they never will." I reach out and take his hand. "I hope you understand."

He nods, and Farkas opens the door, followed by Renata and Zoe.

"Zsuzsa, your turn."

I nod to Farkas, squeeze Peter's hand, and walk into the room.

Lili sits on a chair with the camera set up on a tripod in front of her. She comes forward and hugs me, then has me sit on the chair beside her.

"Zsuzsa, just talk to me, okay? Don't even worry about the camera. I'll ask you questions; all you have to do is answer."

I nod, and she smiles. She looks at a notecard in her hand, then back up at me. "Ready?"

"Yes."

She looks at Farkas, and he turns on the camera.

"Will you state your name, please?"

"Yes. My name is Másik Zsuzsa."

"Do you mind if I call you Zsuzsa?"

"Not at all."

"Zsuzsa, I understand you work as a manager of a local restaurant in Budapest. Is that right?"

"Yes."

"And I understand your former employer was a human trafficker?"

"Yes, his name was Dobo Andras."

"How did you learn of his trafficking young girls?"

"Well, we had many young women who would work in the restaurant, then just disappear. One day, I asked him about it, and he threatened me. He told me to keep my mouth shut, or I would disappear also."

"Did anything else happen to you with your employer?"

"No. After that, I never asked him again. But, one day, I walked out of the restaurant early. I saw Andras talking with a tall man. He drove a car with government license plates."

Lili holds up a photo of Director Toth. "Was it this man?"

"Yes."

"Do you know him?"

"I do now."

"Did they see you?"

"Yes. Andras was mad that I came out there, and Director Toth got in his car and drove away. I never saw him again."

"I understand you were abducted shortly after that?"

"Yes." I tell Lili about my experience working in the club and being abducted. I tell her about Agoston, the club manager holding me there and getting a call from an inside source, knowing help was coming.

After finishing my story, she thanks me, and Farkas turns off the camera.

I walk out of the room and exit the house, blinking against the sunshine. I take several deep breaths and feel a sense of relief. The relief is short-lived, however. My mind drifts back to Peter. I wasn't completely honest with him. I love him, and my feelings about him are unchanged. My hesitation isn't that I need time. My doubts are that I don't believe he can be what I want. When I was with Gabor, I loved his attention. He wanted to be with me, and he showed me. I knew I meant something to him. Maybe it was an act, but it still felt good. Peter has been the opposite. He always seems to have other things on his mind. I want a relationship where I'm number one to him, and he's number one to me. I lean over the railing on the front porch and feel tears well up in my eyes. If only he could be what I want him to be.

Chapter Forty-Six

Peter

After Zsuzsa finishes and leaves the room, she exits the house. Peter wonders if she's okay but knows he's not who she needs. He decides to give her space. He goes into the room where Farkas and Lili are talking.

"What do you think?" Peter asks.

Farkas shakes his head. "The interviews were compelling, but I don't think they prove Director Toth is the head of the trafficking syndicate. I just don't think we have enough."

"Really?" Lili exclaims.

Farkas frowns. "Really."

Peter sighs. "I have an idea. Leave the camera setup."

He walks out of the room, through the kitchen, and into the adjacent room. Varga sits on the ground, her back against the wall. Her hands are still shackled behind her back, her feet tied at the ankles. Peter walks over and sits down beside her. He reaches over and removes the tape from her mouth.

"How are you doing, Detective?"

Varga says nothing, ignoring his presence.

Peter leans his back against the wall and looks up at the ceiling. "Did your father know?"

Varga doesn't react immediately but eventually turns and looks at him. "What?"

"That his stepbrother was a trafficker? That you were working with him?"

She looks away from Peter and stares at the ground. "No."

"What do you think his reaction is going to be?"

Varga doesn't look up. She continues staring at the ground.

Peter exhales. "I can't imagine how he'll feel."

She doesn't react, but he knows he's getting to her.

"You're his only daughter, right?"

She remains still, but he already knows the answer.

"I had a daughter. She passed away several years ago. She meant everything to her mother and me. For years, we tried to have children but were unsuccessful. Then, one day, when we'd lost hope, we found out my wife was pregnant. Six months later, our daughter was born. She was the most beautiful thing I'd ever seen. My love for her was endless. I remember holding her in my arms for the first time. I couldn't love anything more."

Peter straightens his legs and looks back up at the ceiling.

"When she was almost a year old, my wife went into her room one morning to wake her. She couldn't. She was rushed to the hospital, and we learned she had a brain tumor. She entered emergency surgery, and they were able to remove the tumor. Weeks later, we were able to take our daughter home. Things got back to normal, and our lives went on. Our daughter grew, and she began to walk and talk. I'll never forget the first time she said, *Dada*."

Peter smiles, and Varga watches him intently. He's reaching her.

"Two years later, we could tell something wasn't right. We took her back to the hospital, and they found more cancer. Our little girl battled for months but eventually succumbed to the plague that had ripped through her body."

Peter turns and looks Varga in the eye.

"Not a day goes by that I don't think about my daughter. I miss her terribly. I think about your father in all this. He'll feel the betrayal from what you and your uncle did. You'll never be able to make up for it; you'll be in prison for years, but you *can* do something for him. You can tell your story to help ease the pain he'll suffer."

Peter nods and pushes himself up.

"I'll give you five minutes. Think about it."

Chapter Forty-Seven

Director Toth

Past

"Sir, table for one?"

"No, someone else will be joining me."

"Very good."

The pretty, young hostess with captivating eyes grabs another menu and bids me to follow. I walk behind her until she stops at a table for two near the windows.

"Is this okay?"

I nod, and she hands me the menu after I sit.

She walks away, and I take a moment to survey the restaurant. My eyes are drawn to the beautiful blonde behind the bar. It's clear why the only occupied seats are surrounding her. She smiles and laughs with her customers, who are enraptured by her. A young man in a crisp white shirt and black trousers exits the kitchen and comes around the bar straight for me.

"Good afternoon, sir. My name is Attila. I'll be taking care of you today. Are we waiting for one more?"

"Yes."

"Very good. Would you like anything to drink while you wait?"

"Can you bring a bottle of your finest champagne?"

"Certainly."

He leaves, and I go back to watching the bartender when I sense someone standing beside me. He's a large man with dark hair tinged with the first signs of gray and a broad smile.

"Thank you for coming in today," he says, extending his hand. "My name is Dobo Andras, head chef and owner."

I look him in the eye and take his hand.

"I don't think I've seen you here before. Who do I have to thank for the referral?"

"My son. He came in a few weeks back and has raved about it ever since."

Andras smiles more broadly. "What's his name? I'd love to thank him."

I look down at my watch, then back up at him. "He'll be here soon. You can thank him then."

"Excellent! When he arrives, I'll come by again. Enjoy your meal."

"Thank you."

He leaves, and I look up at the TV. The sound is off, but the closed captioning is on. Árpád Göncz, the president of the Republic of Hungary, is having a press conference. I can tell it's live because I recognize his tie from our meeting earlier.

"Sorry, I'm late," my son says as he sits down across from me.

I can tell he's anxious. He knows how much I detest tardiness. But I'm not angry. Not today. I don't think anything could upset me now.

"It's fine. I remember how difficult being a new officer can be."

I see the surprise in his eyes. He was expecting to get a butt chewing.

The server returns and places a bottle of champagne in an ice bucket on the table, along with two glasses.

"Welcome," he says to my son, then turns back to me. "Anything else right now?"

"No, we'll be ready to order in a few minutes."

"Very good."

He walks away, and my son, Máté, gives me a curious look.

I ignore it, open the champagne, and pour each of us a glass.

"Dad? What's the occasion?"

I pick up my glass, put it in front of me, and smile. "Aren't you going to toast your old man?"

He frowns. "Why?"

"Do you need a reason? I'm your father."

He picks up his glass, and I can see he's trying to come up with something to say.

"I just came from a meeting with the president."

"Of Hungary?"

"Yes."

"Why?"

"I wanted you to be the first to hear. I'm going to be made director of the National Police."

His eyes go wide before he smiles at me. "Wow! Congratulations."

"Thank you."

"When?"

"It'll be announced this week."

He nods, and I can see he's taking in the implications of the news. "What does that mean for me?"

"What do you mean?"

"I mean, now you'll be my boss. I should say you'll be my boss's boss's boss." He chuckles.

"Oh, I don't imagine anything will change there. But if you're ever unhappy, you let me know."

He smiles, nods, and raises his glass. "To you, Director Toth. May you have a long and fruitful reign."

He chuckles, and I smile. We each take a drink; then I pick up my menu.

"So, what do you recommend?"

The owner, Andras, comes back to the table. "Máté," he says, extending his hand. "I was talking to your father earlier; I understand I have you to thank for his visit."

Máté smiles. "I told him it was the best food I've had in a long time."

Andras touches his shoulder. "Ah, you're too kind."

"I asked Máté this, but I might as well ask you—what's your favorite? What would you recommend?"

His eyes narrow as he looks at me. I can see he's determining what might fit me. "You look like a traditional man. Someone who loves our country and enjoys the classics. I'd recommend the töltött paprika." Stuffed peppers.

I can't help the smile that creeps across my face while Máté laughs.

"How did you do that? That's his favorite dish in the whole world."

Andras winks and points to Máté. "And what will you be having, sir?"

"Well, if you can predict his favorite, I want you to choose mine."

Andras nods and reaches for our menus. He turns to leave when Máté calls after him. Andras stops but doesn't turn around. "Hey, so what am I getting?"

Andras turns only his head. "Patience, young Officer Toth, patience." He continues his confident stride toward the kitchen.

The young hostess who had seated me earlier walks by him. She looks up at him, admiration dripping from her eyes. She heads back to her post at the front of the restaurant and doodles on a notepad. She can't wipe the grin from her face.

An idea percolates in my mind.

Chapter Forty-Eight

Peter

"What's got you so down?"

Peter turns and looks at Tom, but his eyes are on the highway. They've only been on the road two minutes after pulling out from Tom's sister's driveway, intending to return to Budapest. "What are you talking about?"

"You know what I'm talking about. Since this morning, you've been moping around like someone stole your teddy bear. Now, who stole it?"

Peter looks out the window and says in a low voice, "Zsuzsa."

Tom glances over at him. "She told you, huh?"

Peter turns and frowns at him.

"She told you she's in love with me?" Tom jokes.

Peter shakes his head.

"I told her it was too soon. I told her you wouldn't be able to handle it yet."

Peter doesn't smile and turns back to gazing out the passenger window.

"What did she say?"

"I asked her if we could do that date we missed out on when I was arrested. She turned me down."

"Why?"

"She said she's not ready for a relationship. She said the Gabor thing really affected her. She wants time for herself. Oh, and she also thinks I'm not ready. She tried to let me down easy, but it was clear she was no longer interested."

Tom says nothing and continues to drive. After five minutes, he clears his throat and says, "Peter, have I ever told you I was in a concentration camp?"

Peter turns and frowns at him. "A better question is, when have we ever had a discussion without you bringing it up."

Tom looks at him and smiles. "Oh, good, so I've mentioned it. Well, as you might remember, I left a girl in London to return to Hungary. The war started, and I was thrown into a concentration camp. I regret leaving. I never should have come back to Hungary. If I'd stayed in London, we'd be married, and I'd have never lived through that nightmare. I don't know what else would be different, but I sure would have saved myself some heartache."

They look at each other, then Tom adds, "Fight for her, brother. Show her how much you care. My guess is she doesn't know and won't until you show her."

Twenty minutes later, Peter tells Tom to pull to the side of the road. He can see the flash of police lights ahead. Once they're stopped, he puts his hand on the door handle, but before turning it, he looks back at Tom.

"I've got the tape," Peter says.

Tom nods.

"Whatever you do, don't let them know about me. Toth may have given them my photo. You'll pick me up in Budakeszi?"

"I'll be there."

Peter gets out of the van and walks off the side of the road into the field. He wonders how far he needs to go from the road before he can start heading east again. After all the interviews were done this morning, they watched Duna Television and Director Toth's press conference. In addition to learning Szabo was dead, they heard Toth blame Farkas and institute a national manhunt for him. Toth had made a mistake informing the press they would search vehicles in and out of Budapest. All Peter needs to do is walk several miles until he reaches Budakeszi, and Tom will pick him back up.

Chapter Forty-Nine

Director Toth

Past

Since going to Szep Illona's for the first time with Máté, I've been back a couple more times. Each time, Andras comes by to greet me. The last time, he offered his condolences. He had heard about Máté. I accepted them and thanked him. Losing my son was one of the most difficult pills I've ever had to swallow. Just like the first time, the food failed to disappoint. But it's not the food that drew me back. It's Andras. He's exactly what I need: tall, handsome, charismatic, and desperate. Not desperate in the traditional sense. Not sexually. He's desperate to save a sinking business. Only someone who has been desperate can see such desperation in someone else.

Although the food and atmosphere are fantastic, people aren't coming in sufficient quantities. If he isn't losing money, he certainly isn't making much profit. Someone can only make so much investment until life's needs pop up. He needs a lifeline.

A man exits the glass doors before me, sees me, and holds the door. We smile and nod to each other as I enter. Naturally, he's an older man. What a difference. If he were thirty years younger, he'd let the door swing closed in my face. The younger generation has no respect.

I walk into the lobby of the headquarters of Nemzeti Bank in Budapest and look around. All six teller windows and five small desks with cubicle walls are occupied. A line of at least two people stands in front of each teller window. I pick one of the lines and wait my turn. After five minutes, a teller speaks to me.

"*Jó napot. Hogyan segithetek?*" (Good day. How can I help you?)

"Yes, my name is Toth József." I slide my card under the window. She picks it up and looks at it. "I'd like to speak with the owner, if possible."

She examines the card, then looks back up at me. "Is something the matter, sir?"

"Not at all. I'd just like a few minutes of his time."

She nods and asks me to wait while she scurries off. I watch her speak with a middle-aged man. Her back is to me, and the man glances in my direction several times. After a brief conversation, she returns and tells me her manager will speak to me. I thank her as she points to his desk in the lobby. He stands as I approach.

"Mr. Toth, thank you for coming in today."

"Thank you. I'd like to speak with your boss."

"Is he expecting you?"

"No."

"Very good. Let me go see if he's available. Would you mind waiting here?"

I sit in a chair opposite his desk as he walks away. Before long, he returns.

"Mr. Toth, Mr. Zsigmond will see you. Would you mind following me?"

"Thank you."

He walks me to the elevator. When we enter, he pushes the button to the fourth floor and then steps back. He's tapping his foot and nervously wringing his hands. He looks at me and smiles. I keep my face impassive. When we reach the fourth floor, he steps out first, extends his palm, and guides me to the office. We walk down a hallway where a woman sits at a desk. She looks at me and then back to the manager. "He's expecting you."

The manager opens the office door, and I follow him. The bank owner sits behind his large mahogany desk but stands when we enter. He comes around the corner with his hand extended. "Director Toth, this is an unexpected honor."

"Mr. Zsigmond," I say, taking his hand. He's a little man, not more than five feet six inches. I tower over him and the manager.

"Thank you, Zsolt." He looks at the manager to dismiss him, then turns back to me. "Please, sit down."

I sit in the plush chair opposite the desk. Mr. Zsigmond sits next to me rather than return to his customary chair.

"How can I help you, Director?"

"I have a favor to ask."

The slight retract of his head tells me he's surprised by my abruptness. "Okay, I'll do what I can."

"I understand a man named Dobo Andras has come to you seeking a loan for his restaurant."

He shakes his head. "Sir, I'm not involved in most loan requests. I can't confirm or deny that."

"You don't have to. I already know it's true."

"Okay."

"I want you to deny the loan."

"Has he done something wrong? Something illegal?"

"No. I have reasons for the request that I'd rather not share. I'm asking as a personal favor. As you probably know, I have a sizeable amount of money on deposit in your institution. I'd hate to move that money somewhere else."

If he was surprised before, the whiteness of his eyes demonstrates his shock now. "I understand. I'll see that the loan is denied."

"Thank you, Mr. Zsigmond. I appreciate that. If I can do something for you in the future, please don't hesitate to reach out."

"Thank you, sir."

I stand, and he shows me to the door. He walks me to the elevator. After he presses the call button, I say, "Also, once he knows the loan has been denied, I'd like a phone call notifying me."

"Certainly. I'll call you myself."

"Thank you."

I shake his hand and enter the elevator. As I leave the bank, the bank manager smiles and waves. I nod, exit the building, and turn south toward my office. Soon, Andras will work for me, and I'll have a new operation in a different vertical. For the first time since the fall of communism, I feel invincible.

Chapter Fifty

Peter

Tom makes a left on Kunigunda Útca while Peter surveys the street.

"That's it," Peter says, pointing to the building across the road. "Keep going. Let's make certain the coast is clear."

Tom reduces his speed as Peter examines the cars parked along the route.

"Yep, they're watching the building."

"How do you know?"

"You didn't see the guy sitting in the green Opel across the street from the television station?"

"Do you want a driver or a spy? I don't do both. You don't pay me enough."

Peter chuckles and shakes his head. "Just go around the corner up here."

Tom puts on his blinker while Peter sits rubbing his beard.

"Find a parking spot."

Tom drives halfway up the road, then locates one. It's not pretty, and it takes him several tries, but finally, he manages to parallel park on the street. He kills the engine and looks at Peter.

"Now what?"

Peter opens the glove box and pulls out a map of Budapest. "How do you feel about asking for directions?"

"Directions to where?"

"Wherever you want."

Tom frowns.

"We need a distraction. Something to pull the guy's eyes off the front door so I can go inside without being seen."

Peter unfolds the map and expands it.

"This is perfect. Hold it up high so he can't see the building. I'll hide around the corner. Once I see it go up, I'll sneak in. Be the bumbling idiot. You're good at that, right?"

Tom laughs while Peter refolds the map and hands it to him.

"Why are they watching the building? How could Toth possibly know?"

"He doesn't. But he knows he controls everything in the city other than the press. It's the only thing that can hurt him. With Varga gone and Farkas at large, he's taking no chances. I bet he has someone watching all the major newspaper and television offices."

Tom nods, and Peter opens the passenger door.

"I'll meet you back here when I'm done."

"How are you going to get out without being seen?"

"I'm not sure yet. I'll figure that out later. A lot has to go right before then."

Peter circles the block and waits behind a corner, one building away from the headquarters of Duna Television. After a couple of minutes, he sees Tom walk along the sidewalk. He holds the map with a dumbfounded look. He stops in front of the green Opel, looks for the street sign, then throws his hands in the air. Peter can't hear the words, but he can bet Tom's let loose a stream of profanity. He looks back down at the map and then at the man in the Opel. Peter chuckles at the look on Tom's face. Tom approaches the car and motions for the man to roll down his window. The man complies, and Tom holds up the map, pointing to it.

Peter takes that as his cue. He quickly strides to the building, climbs the small steps, and ducks inside. He can only hope Tom held the man's attention. He rings for the elevator and exits once he's reached the fourth floor. A large electric sign hangs above the reception desk with the words *Duna Televízió*. Peter approaches the woman sitting behind the desk.

"Hello, can I please speak with Böröcz Attila?"

"Do you have an appointment?"

"No, but I bring a message from Horváth Lili."

She shakes her head. "Horváth Lili doesn't work here anymore."

"Exactly. He's going to want to hear what happened to her."

The woman raises an eyebrow but says nothing. She picks up the phone on her desk and presses a button. "Mr. Böröcz, there's a man here to see you who says he knows what happened to Horváth Lili." She nods several times, then whispers into the phone. She puts it back down when she's finished and looks at Peter. "Mr. Böröcz will see you."

Peter follows her as she guides him through the newsroom. They reach Böröcz's office, and Peter thanks her when she introduces them.

Böröcz glares at him. "Have a seat; you have five minutes."

"I'll need a VCR and TV. It's better if I show you."

"You've come to the right place for that."

Böröcz stands and motions for Peter to follow. They walk through the newsroom and enter a small dark room with a couple of producers inside with headsets on. There's a switchboard in front of them and several TV monitors with different camera angles of the same woman on the screen. She's sitting behind a desk.

"István, is there a VCR and TV I can use?"

He holds up a finger, presses something on the switchboard, then turns to Böröcz. "What?"

"A VCR. Is there one I can use?"

He points to the other side of the room. Böröcz walks over, takes the tape from Peter, and pops it in. He hands Peter a set of headphones as Böröcz puts on his own. Horváth Lili, his former employee, comes on the screen sitting in Tom's sister's house.

"Attila, as you know, I interviewed a girl on air named Agnes. She was killed, which resulted in my termination from Duna Television. I deeply regret my actions. My choice to put her on air resulted in her death. I'll have to live with that shame for the rest of my life."

The producer sitting to Böröcz's right smacks his arm, points to Lili, then gestures with his palms up in a "what's going on?" motion.

Böröcz ignores him and turns back to Lili.

"On this tape, I interview six different people. Each of them shares incriminating evidence of corruption, extortion, and murder. The man they identify has long been running a sex-trafficking syndicate in Hungary, specifically Budapest. This man is none other than Director Toth József, head of the Hungarian National Police. Peter, the man who has brought you this tape, is one of the individuals I interviewed. He was a consultant on the human trafficking task force for the National Police. He was the first to identify Mr. Toth's corruption."

Böröcz turns and looks at Peter, then back to the screen.

"My interviews begin with Julia, a cashier from an internet café in Budapest. Next comes Zsuzsa, a bartender who worked in a restaurant owned by a trafficker working for Mr. Toth. After Zsuzsa comes Renata, a girl abducted from a Budapest nightclub and best friend to Agnes, the girl I interviewed before. After Renata comes Detective Farkas, an employee of Toth's and a human-trafficking-task-force member. Next is Peter, the man who brought you the tape, then Detective Varga, Toth's niece and task force member.

What you're about to hear is both shocking and abhorrent. Mr. Toth's corruption is beyond belief. As you may know, I collaborated with a man from the *Magyar Hirlap* newspaper, Nagy Béla. He was working on this story and was murdered by Toth. In his honor, I ask that you release this story in conjunction with the *Magyar Hirlap*, and Béla is cited as a contributor. He gave his life to expose Toth and stop the trafficking."

Böröcz pushes stop on the machine while removing his headphones. He stares at Peter.

"I want as many people to see this as possible."

Chapter Fifty-One

Peter

Peter sits at the head of the conference table at Duna Television's headquarters. The room is full of news reporters, interns, camera operators, executives, etc. Böröcz Attila, the program director, stands by the TV in the center of the room. Böröcz is explaining to the gathering what Lili had said in the opening statements of the tape. Wide eyes and dropped jaws are prevalent throughout the room. When he's done, he presses play and takes a seat. Everyone watches as Lili interviews each of the witnesses. Peter notices people glancing at him when he comes on screen. Finally, they reach Detective Varga. Although her hands and feet remain shackled, Peter's relieved to see it's not apparent on camera.

"Hello, will you tell me your name?" Lili says.

"My name is Németh Nádja, but I've gone by Detective Varga Naómi for several years."

"Do you mind if I call you Detective Varga?"

"No."

"Detective Varga, where do you work?"

"I work as a detective for the Hungarian National Police in the human-trafficking task force."

"Who is your boss there?"

"Director Toth József."

"But he's more than a boss for you, right?"

"Yes."

"How else do you know him?"

"He's my father's stepbrother and the head of the human trafficking syndicate in Hungary."

"And you work for him in the syndicate?"

"Yes."

"How long have you been working for him there?"

"Four years."

"How did you start?"

"His son, my cousin Máté, and I started at the academy at the same time. I legally changed my name to Varga to prevent any accusations of nepotism. After graduating from the academy, the director met with us. That's when he told us about the trafficking. He took over the business with the help of my grandfather, the former mayor of Újpest. He offered us an opportunity to get involved, promising we'd be in charge one day."

"And what was your reaction to this?"

"He spoke of the money we could make, and I was excited. Especially knowing my family had been involved in it for years."

"What was Máté's reaction?"

"Abhorrence. He condemned his father and threatened him. He said he'd expose him to his mother and everyone else unless the director confessed."

"What happened next?"

"The director ordered me to kill Máté."

"And did you?"

"Yes. Máté was called to a staged robbery in Újpest, where I was waiting for him. His partner, another member of the trafficking syndicate, left him alone while I shot him."

"What happened after that?"

"I'd shown my loyalty to my uncle. He trusted me and made me his right hand. I was involved in everything, and he paid me generously."

"You were involved in trafficking the girls?"

"Yes. I paid the club owners or whoever else we hired to acquire the product."

"Did Mr. Toth order you to kill anyone else while working for him?"

"Yes."

"Who?"

"A few different people who worked in the syndicate and displeased the director. More recently, Detective Kovacs Lajos, Andrassy Peter, and Agnes, the girl you interviewed on TV."

"You killed all those people?"

"Yes. Well, not Peter. I tried but only got Detective Kovacs. After that, the plan was to kill Peter in jail, but he was released before he could be murdered."

Everyone in the room looks at Peter.

"Why are you telling us all this? Are you being forced?"

"No."

"Then, why?"

"For my father, Németh László, the mayor of Újpest. People are going to think he was involved. He knew nothing about it. People need to know that."

"Why was he not the one made leader of the syndicate? Why was it your uncle?"

"My grandfather approached him, but my father refused. My uncle never told my father about his involvement."

"Is there anything else you'd like to say?"

"I'm sorry. I'm sorry to those I hurt. I'm ashamed of my actions." She looks down, then back up and into the camera. "Dad, I'm so sorry."

"Thank you for telling us."

The screen goes black, and there's silence in the room. Böröcz turns to his secretary.

"Get me the *Nemzeti Hirlap* on the phone."

Fifteen minutes later, after hanging up with the newspaper, Böröcz shouts commands to his people. He gives the tape to his video editors and gets them working on splitting up portions of the interviews. He talks to his lead reporter and anchors about special report headlines and locations. Finally, he turns to Peter. "Anything else you need from me?"

"Yes. What's the headroom situation in your car's trunk?"

Chapter Fifty-Two

Peter

Peter feels the bumping of the car stop and hears a door open. A key is inserted into the lock, and Böröcz Attila stands over him, hand extended. Peter takes the extended hand and climbs out of the trunk.

"You sure I can't take you anywhere else?"

"No, I'm fine here." Attila nods. "When's the news going to break?"

"Sometime tomorrow morning. It'll be a late night. There's a lot to coordinate with the newspaper."

Peter nods. "Good luck."

Attila shakes his head. "I'm a news guy. I live for this. This will be the biggest story of my life."

"I do have one more request for you."

"Shoot."

"Rehire Lili. Give her a job again. Maybe not as a shopping queen but as an actual reporter. She brought you your biggest story."

He looks at Peter, then shrugs. "I'll see what I can do."

"I mean it."

Attila shakes his head. "Her careless actions caused a girl's death and a likely lawsuit for the station."

"And she brought you the biggest story of your career."

He nods, but Peter knows he hasn't convinced him.

"You're, what, fifty?"

"Fifty-one."

"Did you ever do anything you regret in your twenties?"

Attila stares at him, knowing where he's going.

"Wouldn't you appreciate a do-over? She's a gifted journalist who's learned a hard lesson. Give her a chance to make up for it."

He sighs. "You make a strong point. I'll fight for her."

"Thank you."

They shake hands, and Attila returns to the car while Peter walks away. Peter doesn't have to walk far, only a block, when he arrives at the white van with the aroma of cigarette smoke. He opens the passenger door, and Tom jumps, knocking ash all over his clothes.

"I told you not to smoke in the van."

"What? The window is down. Plus, it's been hours. What took so long?"

Peter smiles. "We're set. It's going to break in the morning."

"Good. I'm tired."

"Speaking of. Why don't you head home and get a few hours of sleep? Then I'd appreciate it if you could return to Tatabánya and wait with everyone until I give you the all-clear."

"Okay. What about you?"

"I need to find a rental car."

Chapter Fifty-Three

Director Toth

Present

The phone buzzes on my desk, and I pick it up.

"Yes."

"Sir, they're ready for you."

"Okay, I'll be right down. Give me five minutes."

I stand from my desk and walk to the tie rack. Blue. This is my favorite tie. It's royal blue with a black checkered pattern. I slide it off the shelf, pop my collar, and wrap the tie around my neck. I pause and look in the mirror. The years are showing. On days like this, when I haven't slept, it's more apparent. Lines surround my eyes, and the wrinkles in my forehead are more pronounced. *Is it as evident to everyone else as it is to me?*

Last night, when I arrived home late, Eszter was already in bed, her back turned to me. Her empty bourbon glass lay on its side on the nightstand. Once again, she drank herself to sleep. When we first married, she'd wait until I got home. No matter how late. She'd ask about my day and tell me about hers. When did that change? Máté. It changed with Máté. After he was killed, she began drinking more heavily. She couldn't bear the heartbreak.

As I lay there, listening to her steady snoring, I thought about going to Ildiko, my only remaining child. I hadn't seen her in a week. I often arrive home after bedtime, and I'm gone again before she wakes. She's fourteen and a full-on teenager. I wonder if she even notices.

I return to the present and stare at my reflection in the mirror. I know why I couldn't sleep. I don't understand what Farkas is doing. He has Varga and the bartender. He likely has the girl from the internet café, too. I can't understand what his play is. By now, I would have thought he'd reach out. Try and negotiate. Is Varga still alive? Has she talked? Is anyone helping him?

The only potential help is Peter. My contact in the United States lost track of Peter weeks ago. Did he come back? I shake my head. No, that's impossible. How would he? I'd know. Border control knows I'm to be alerted if his passport ever crosses our borders again. Peter's still in the United States. He must be.

I finish with my tie and walk out of my office. I head down the hall and push open the glass door. I look down at the congregation below. There's more press than I've ever seen at one of my press conferences. I sigh and walk to the steps. I'd rather not do this today.

My nephew, Ferenc, steps out of my way when I reach the lower level and says nothing. Hmm, that's odd. Usually, he greets me and lays out the agenda. Is it my eyes? My look? Can he sense my exhaustion and foul temperament? I step to the podium and wait for the crowd to quiet.

"Unfortunately, I don't have too much to report today. As of right now, Mr. Farkas has alluded capture. We believe he's still here in the city, armed and dangerous. Our tip line is still open, and blockades will remain on all highways and freeways in and out of Budapest. We're investigating all leads and hope to make an arrest soon. If there are any questions, I'll take them now."

A young man I recognize from the *Nemzeti Hirlap* raises his hand. Unlike any other press conference I've done before, he's the only one. No other hands go up. Nobody shouts for me to call on them. I'm taken aback as I point at him. Perhaps a press conference was unnecessary today. But if that's true, why the vast crowd?

"Director, do you have any comment about the story on the front page of *the Nemzeti Hirlap*?"

I shake my head. "I'm sorry. I don't have time for reading newspapers right now."

He holds up a copy, and I see a large photo of myself with a caption in bold letters: Head of the National Police Accused of Murder, Trafficking, and Corruption.

I frown and look around at the multitude of faces watching me. My eyes fall on Ferenc. He wheels out a television set, and a TV anchor appears. I've seen her before. She's the lead anchor on Duna Television. All eyes move from me to the screen as Ferenc turns the volume to maximum.

"Breaking news this morning. Toth József, director of the National Police Force of Hungary, has been accused of human trafficking, corruption, and murder. Duna Television has obtained firsthand accounts of the director's despicable acts. Horváth Lili sat down with his accusers to hear their stories firsthand."

My eyes remain transfixed to the screen as Varga is the first to appear with Lili. My mouth drops open as she details the killing of Detective Kovacs and Béla, the newspaper reporter. She also talks about her own guilt in the trafficking syndicate. I feel eyes on me and look at the crowd of people. Their gaze has moved from the TV screen back to me. A young woman in the front with a Duna Television credential shouts at me.

"Director, five other witnesses have firsthand accounts of your murderous actions. What do you have to say to these accusations?"

I back away from the podium and feel someone behind me. I whirl around, raising my gun. An officer lifts his hands above his head as people scream and scatter. I point the gun at his head as he holds his hands high, terror in his eyes. I spin back around, my gun aimed before me, expecting to see other guns pointed at me, but there are none. People lie on the floor around me while others run for the exit. I keep my gun trained on the crowd as I move back toward the exit leading to the garage. When I reach it, I turn and bolt through the door.

Chapter Fifty-Four

Director Toth

Present

I run through the parking garage, looking back over my shoulder. Nobody's following me. I swing my head back and forth, expecting uniformed officers to pop out with guns drawn. But they don't. I'm alone. Why would they let me go? I reach my car and unlock the door. I slide into the sleek black Audi with rich leather seats and power everything. I turn the ignition, rev the engine, and reverse. I shift to first gear and drive as fast as I dare through the narrow driveway. As I near the parking attendant, he raises the gate without hesitation. This seems too easy. Shouldn't they try and stop me?

Then, it comes to me with perfect clarity. Those orders would come from me. If I'm not giving them, who would? They're confused. They don't know who to follow. I pull in front of a bus, and it wins me a chorus of honks and squealing tires. I head west, toward the river and Buda. I'm not sure where I'm going. I just know I need distance. The light turns red, but I ignore it, mashing the gas. Cars on either side of the intersection pull forward as I buzz past them. The horn blasts begin again, but they're the least of my worries.

Before I reach the river, I turn left on Balassi Bálint Utca and head south. I continue south, passing the Parliament Building before I can get to the frontage road along the river's east side. I pass under the Chain Bridge and the Elizabeth Bridge until I near the Freedom Bridge.

Szabadság, or Freedom, was the third bridge built in Budapest. It's the shortest bridge that spans the river and only has one lane of traffic heading in either direction. A streetcar track runs through the center, splitting the lanes. On the west side of the bridge sits the Gellert Hotel, and beyond that, south Buda. I want out of Budapest, and this is the easiest way for me to reach my destination. As I accelerate onto the bridge, my eyes narrow on the scene before me. A blockade has been constructed on the west side. I stop in the middle and look in my rearview mirror. Police vehicles are lining up on the east side behind me. I'm trapped. I look to the north, to the Elizabeth Bridge. I don't know how I missed it before, but the same blockade is arranged on the west side of that bridge. They wanted me to come to the bridges. It's the perfect trap.

I look back and forth to the west and east. There's no way I could ram through them, not in an Audi. I pick up my gun from the passenger seat and exit the car. I'm alone on the bridge except for a red Volkswagen sedan parked a couple hundred feet behind me. I walk south, across the streetcar tracks, to the edge of the bridge. I climb through the green metal railing and look down at the dirty water below. I must be two hundred feet above the water.

The city's silent. Almost peaceful. I hear nothing but my heart pounding as I look at my watery tomb below. How could it come to this? I think back on all I've accomplished. All I've done. I was an orphaned child of factory workers who rose up to be one of the country's most influential and wealthy men. Now, unless I jump, I face a life of prison bars and misery. I'll be sharing the same prisons as the men I sent there. I won't last a day. If I jump, at least I go out under my terms.

A click of a pistol hammer sounds behind me. I turn, raising my gun.

Andrassy Peter stands east of me, his gun pointed at my chest.

"Step away from the edge."

I look at him and smile. "Why? So you can parade me around the city? Make me face my accusers? Let my victims lash out at me?" I shake my head and laugh. "No thanks, Peter. I'll take my chances with the river."

It happens so fast I don't have time to react. He moves the aim of his gun from my chest to my thigh and fires. My leg buckles and I feel searing pain emanating from my quad. I look down to see blood pooling under my pant leg. My eyes rise back up as I look at him in shock.

"Don't make me shoot the other one." Peter aims his gun at my good leg.

I have trouble maintaining my balance as I shift the weight of my body to the left leg. No! I won't let him take me. I raise my gun, but instead of pointing it toward him, I place it under my chin and look him in the eye before pulling the trigger. "You know, Peter, you're always going to be chasing the wicked."

Chapter Fifty-Five

Peter

Peter stands with his gun still aimed at the director. He's just fired a bullet into Toth's leg and prepares to shoot the other when Toth raises his weapon. Peter shifts the aim of his pistol up toward the director's chest when Toth places the gun under his chin, says something, and fires. Blood spurts out of the top of his head as the bullet passes through. Toth's eyes go white as they roll back in his head, his body falling. Peter steps forward but is too far away. The director's body flips over the railing and plummets to the river below. Toth's gun rattles to the ground as Peter rushes to the edge, just as Toth's body hits the water.

Peter leans over the railing, his eyes glued to the scene below as he hears sirens and the squeal of tires. Within seconds, he's surrounded by police officers. Detective Katona, the only remaining member of the human trafficking task force, places a hand on his shoulder. "Come on, let's head back to the station."

Peter sits at the small conference table adjacent to the task force bullpen an hour later. It's the same conference room he'd sat in on his first day as a consultant to the National Police. He sips a cup of hot tea and looks out the window.

The door opens behind him. Farkas enters the room, followed by Zsuzsa, Renata, Zoe, Julia, Lili, and Tom. He stands as they approach him one by one and hug him. They form a crescent shape in front of him. He smiles, a bit embarrassed, as they all smile back. Tears stream down the faces of Renata, Zoe, and Julia. Farkas looks at Lili and nods.

"Peter," she says. Her words catch in her throat. "We all want you to know how grateful we are. You've saved each of our lives." She chuckles. "Some of us more than once. None of us will ever be able to repay that debt. But we want you to know how much we love and appreciate you."

Peter looks at each person, each smiling face, and he can't deny the joy he feels in his heart. He thinks back to almost a year and a half ago when he had stepped off the plane in Budapest after leaving as a sixteen-year-old boy. He thinks about his father and his heartbreak as his father prohibited him from reentering his childhood home. He thinks about Karen and the years they had together. The trials and the happiness. He thinks about his daughter and the joy he had felt when she first smiled at him—the desperation when her cancer returned, and the doctors had no answers. Then Karen was taken from him. When he stepped off that plane in Budapest, returning for the first time since being that boy, he desperately reached for a lifeline. Something that would make him want to live. He could never have dreamed he'd be here, standing in front of these people who mean so much to him.

Seeing Peter is overwhelmed and grasping for something to say, Tom, in his customary way, looks to bring a little levity to the room. He looks at Peter and asks, "You hungry?"

Peter chuckles. "Famished."

"Let's go see if we can find something to eat."

He exits the room, and one by one, each person hugs Peter. Zsuzsa kisses him on the cheek and stares into his eyes before she walks away. Farkas and Katona have arranged rides for each of them, and they hug each other before splitting off. When the women are all gone, it's only Tom, Farkas, and Katona. Peter and Tom start to leave, but Farkas calls out to them.

"Peter, hold on a second." Peter turns and looks at him. "We could still use a consultant around here."

Tom grabs Peter by the arm pulling him away. "He'll get back to you."

Chapter Fifty-Six

Peter

Peter walks along Váci Utca, unaware of the throngs of shoppers milling around the storefronts. After leaving the National Police headquarters, he and Tom ate dinner at a nearby restaurant. Peter could feel the exhaustion overwhelm him as they talked and ate. The day, not to mention the last several months, had been exhausting. Once his belly was full, all he wanted was sleep. Tom felt the same, and they split, agreeing to talk again tomorrow.

Now, Peter reaches his apartment building. As he puts the key in the lock, he thinks how nice it is not to worry about who might see him enter. He begins climbing the stairs when he hears a familiar sound.

"*Kezét csókolom*." His spunky, little nine-year-old neighbor, Judith, calls out from above.

Peter smiles as he looks up at her.

"*Jó estét kívánok*. How are you?"

She smiles. "Where have you been? I've missed you."

Her mother pops her head around the corner. She looks at Peter, rolls her eyes, then speaks to Judith. "Judith, time for bed. You can talk to Peter tomorrow."

"Mom!" she cries.

"I mean it."

Judith shrugs and goes into the apartment. Her mother waves at Peter and wishes him a good night.

He finishes climbing the remaining stairs, enters the dark, lonely apartment, and doesn't bother turning on a light until he reaches the bedroom. He flips on the bedroom light, undresses, and climbs into bed. Before turning out the light, he turns and looks at the picture that sits on his nightstand. Karen and Catherine smile at him. It's his favorite picture in the whole world. He took it during a family outing to Central Park in New York City. Peter winks at them and turns out the light. As he lays in bed, staring at the ceiling, he thinks of who was missing today. Kovacs should have been there, and Szabo. Both men did so much to bring down Toth. He thinks about Agnes. She had her whole life in front of her. How many other victims are there of Toth just like them?

Peter turns in bed and lies on his side. He reaches across the bed to where Karen had been for so many years. The sheets are crisp and cold. His mind drifts back to the central point of the day. For him, it wasn't when Toth had shot himself. It was when Zsuzsa had kissed his cheek and looked into his eyes. It was the same look she had given him when he had first kissed her outside the bar, the look she gave him when they arrived home from Budapest after Ukraine. He can feel his heart rate quicken as he lies there, remembering those eyes.

Chapter Fifty-Seven

Zsuzsa

I arrive early at the restaurant this morning. I love Kata, but she doesn't keep it as tidy as I like, and I know I've got work to do before I feel comfortable opening. I shove my key in the lock and open the door. As I walk through the dining room, sunlight streams through the window. We open at eleven, but I'm here two hours early. I look over at the bar and see splotches. Grrr, Csaba. Before putting down my things, I walk around and run a washcloth through hot water, then rub down the bar. After five minutes, I'm satisfied to the point of being able to leave it. It really needs to be refinished. Age is starting to show.

I glance at the kitchen but look away quickly. I can't look now, or I'll never leave it. I walk down the hallway and enter the office, flipping on the light. I smile as I look at the beautiful landscape painting behind the desk. When this was Andras's office, a massive photo of a wolf hung on the wall. Now, that's been replaced by a beautiful landscape of a mountainous region. I'm not sure where. Maybe Switzerland? I can't get over the crystal-clear water every time I look at it. I wonder if Switzerland really looks like that. Although it's not far from here, I've never been. Maybe someday.

I hang my jacket on the coat rack and put my purse in the cabinet under the desk. There's a scattering of papers. Kata never puts anything away. It's obvious I haven't been in here for days. Poor Kata. She's been running this place on her own while I've been abducted again. At least that should be over. Toth is gone. I can't believe it. No more fearing to walk home. No more worrying about being kidnapped again.

I sit down and exhale, thinking of Gabor. I really haven't had time to process it. His coming here wasn't by accident. I honestly thought he loved me. It hurts to know it was all a ruse. He was sent by Toth to keep an eye on me. I shake my head. I can't think about that right now. I reach to log into the computer, and an envelope on the keyboard stops me.

My name is written on the outside. I don't recognize the handwriting, but it's clearly written by a man. Curious, I open it, unfolding the paper.

Dear Zsuzsa,

I'm sorry for communicating in this way. I couldn't express myself accurately if it were verbal. I'd likely unleash my words in a jumble, and who knows what might come out. At least this way, I can say what I feel in my heart.

I admit, I'm writing to you because I don't need to receive an answer immediately. After bearing my soul, I'm unsure I could handle the rejection if you don't feel the same. Call me a pansy, but this just feels safer.

Zsuzsa, I love you, and what you don't understand is you saved me. I've loved you since I first saw you in this restaurant. I remember walking in and the hostess seating me when I was here to investigate Andras. As I sat at the table, I felt something. I couldn't place it. It was like some magnetic pull in your direction. I thought maybe it was just thirst, but when I looked over and saw you, I knew what it was. It was you, and I had to be near you.

When I approached the bar and sat down, the pull was more powerful. When you talked, when you laughed, I was enchanted. I went home that night, and although I was working two cases at the time, all I could think of was you. Your smile danced around my mind as I lay there trying to sleep. I felt guilty when I woke the next morning after a fitful night of sleep.

As you know, I lost my wife, Karen, only a year earlier. I was ashamed of myself. How could I feel this for another woman? I thought I was being untrue to her. I resolved to remove you from my mind. To banish your eyes from my thoughts. But I had a job to do, and you were part of it, even if you didn't know it. I had to come back and meet Andras. I had to learn more about him. Or at least, that's what I told myself. I knew in my heart I wanted to see you again. I knew I wanted to be near you.

The next time I came in, the pull was every bit as strong. I can't describe what I felt when I looked at you. When you flirted with me, I felt lighter than helium. I couldn't help myself. I had to ask you out. When you said yes, I was intoxicated. I stumbled out of the restaurant and checked my watch every five minutes until I could meet you.

Then we got a drink in that little, shady bar you suggested. You made me laugh; you were so cute. You overwhelmed me. When you rushed out, I panicked. I had to find you. I caught you, and when you turned around, you had tears in your eyes. I wanted so badly to help you. To fix your hurt. Then I kissed you, and you told me about Andras. About who he really was. From that point on, things went at a frenetic pace. Everything seemed to be pulling us apart.

I had more time to think. When I went to Croatia, I wanted to call you. When I came back, I wanted to see you. I thought about you constantly, but the guilt remained. I was hesitant to reach out. I came and saw you and Kata, and I couldn't deny the feelings in my heart.

Then you were abducted. My greatest fear seemed to be realized. My heart couldn't take the thought of another woman I love being taken from me. I was desperate. I went after you in Ukraine without even knowing if you were there. My heart leaped when I came into that old industrial building and saw you. I approached you tentatively, afraid of what I might find. When your eyes opened, and I saw you breathing, I can't describe the relief that washed over me. I can't remember being as happy as I was when we flew home. I knew then we were meant to be together. I kissed you again at the airport as we parted. As I watched you drive away in the taxi, I longed for you. I ached to hold you again.

But, as I'm apt to do, I got inside my own head. I started to worry that I was wrong for you. That being around me was causing you pain and harm. I worried I was putting you in danger. That's why I didn't call. That's why I didn't immediately come to see you. Finally, the desire overtook me, and I came to the restaurant. I understood why you were upset. I was upset with myself. But then you agreed to a date. I was elated.

When I came that night, and Szabo arrested me, I looked up and saw you in the window. I wondered if that would be the last time I would ever see you. Then, a few days later, you came to the jail. The glass felt like an ocean between us. I knew I needed to get out. I had to be with you. But then I heard someone listening to our conversation. Immediately, my concerns came back. I lied to you. I told you I didn't care for you, hoping it would save you. I think it did for a while. I know it was unfair for me to be released and return to America without letting you know, but I had no choice. I knew Toth was watching you.

Then I came back. Yes, I came back to stop Toth, but the truth is I came back for you. You gave me a purpose, a reason to live. You were all I thought about when I reentered the country. I sat outside your apartment, just hoping to see you. I knew I'd never be with you until Toth was apprehended. As I sat, hoping to glimpse you, I saw you with Gabor. I saw him kiss you. I saw you smile as you looked at him. I was devastated. I told myself I just wanted you to be happy, and you were. But it was a lie. I wanted to show you Gabor wasn't what you thought. When he turned out to be, I was both elated and disappointed—disappointed because I knew how it would hurt you.

Why am I telling you all this? Because I recognize my own error. I lost you because of my own stupidity. I know you said we should be friends, but I don't agree. I don't want to be your friend. I want to mean as much to you as you do to me. I want to be with you. I love you. Please give me another chance. I know I'll never truly be whole again unless I'm with you.

    Love,

    Peter

I sit at the desk, transfixed. He said everything I've wanted so badly to hear. My eyes are swimming, and I reach up and wipe the tears with the back of my hand. As I do, I see something move in the doorframe. I turn and see Peter standing there. We stare at each other, neither of us speaking.

Finally, I stand and move toward him.

"I thought you couldn't bear an immediate answer?"

He smiles that delicious smile. "I lied."

"Did you mean what you wrote?"

"Every word."

"I have two questions for you."

"I thought we agreed, one question at a time?"

He's referencing our first date.

I want to smile, but I keep my face serious. "Are you going to continue to think you know what's best for me? Or will you let me decide?"

He smiles again. "I can't wait to let you decide."

I place my hand on his chest. "Good answer. One more. I want someone who's committed to me. I want to be their number one. Can you do that? Will you make me your number one?"

He looks at me, and his smile vanishes. He takes my hand in his. "Zsuzsa, you will be my *only* one."

He steps to me and leans down as I close my eyes, feeling his lips pressed to mine. He wraps his arms around me, and I'm shocked by how much I've missed him. How much I need him. After a few seconds, he releases me, and we stare into each other's eyes.

"How about a date?" he asks.

"When?"

"Right now."

I laugh. "I have to work."

He shakes his head. "No, you don't."

He takes my hand and leads me out of the office to the dining area. Kata sits at a table. When she sees me, she stands and runs over. She throws her arms around me.

"Kata has volunteered to take your shift. I didn't even have to twist her arm. I'm not the only one who loves you."

The End

Afterword

In 2016, I read an article by Ferenc Sullivan titled "Nationwide Campaign Highlights Shocking Number of Missing Children in Hungary." In the article, Ferenc says, "Over 19,000 young people under 18 disappeared in Hungary in 2015, four thousand of whom have not yet been recovered, according to figures released by Hungarian police." The article shocked and sickened me. As you have likely felt in my writing, Hungary holds a special place in my heart. I spent two of the most formative years of my life there, and I have many Hungarian friends. The article and my subsequent research unsettled me. I couldn't let it go.

Around that same time, as I drove home from work one evening, a book idea popped in my head. The idea involved a young, disturbed American graduate student who imagined a girlfriend in an attempt to cope with his anxiety and foreign surroundings. A woman he believed to be real. As I pondered the idea, it became an obsession for me. I had to tell the story, but the missing children in Hungary never left my mind. I considered how I might marry the two subjects.

In 2020, my professional career was heavily impacted by the COVID-19 virus. I work as an event manager for a wonderful company. The lockdowns and public-gathering restrictions prevented us from operating. Events abruptly stopped. I was furloughed for several months and became a tutor to my four sons as they were no longer able to go to school. Suddenly, I had extra time on my hands with no clear idea when I would go back to work.

As long as I can remember, I've dreamed of writing a novel. I believe a well-written novel is a form of immortality for the author. I've long admired novelists and decided to take the plunge and give the story a go.

I spent nine months writing the first draft of *Vanished From Budapest* and, admittedly, had no idea what I was doing. Upon completion, I asked family and friends if they would be willing to read it. Many did and gave me valuable feedback. I also began researching the publishing industry and the craft of writing. I read books, watched countless videos, and attended webinars on writing and publishing. My beta readers told me the story was excellent from the halfway point, but the first half was painfully slow. I hired two different developmental editors and took a class in creative writing. I rewrote the book three times in the process before finally feeling confident it was ready.

My goal was to publish traditionally through a publisher. I thought it would give me the widest distribution. Of course, I wanted to make money from the book, but more than anything, I wanted people to read it. I wanted the story told, and I wanted to raise awareness about the missing children in Hungary. Unless you know someone, and I don't, the only effective way to reach a publishing house for consideration is through a literary agent. I spent hours preparing a query letter and began sending it to agents. I queried nearly one hundred agents with few replies. One actually requested the full manuscript, but after less than a week, emailed and said the story was strong, but there was too much "tell" in my writing and not enough "show." I was devastated and wanted to give up. After several days of contemplation, I resolved to keep trying.

I doubled down on writing education, read books, and watched videos primarily about "show, not tell." After several months and another rewrite, I couldn't bring myself to resume the querying process and began considering self-publishing. I hired another editor and was ecstatic with the positive feedback I received.

On December 10, 2022, I self-published *Vanished From Budapest*. Since then, I've written *Pursuit of Demons, Revealing the Shadows*, and *Chasing the Wicked*. My wife, on a particularly discouraging day, asked me why. Why would I do this? I considered the question and came to two conclusions. One, I enjoy it. I love learning new skills and the pursuit of excellence in everything I do. I'm incredibly proud of my story, and the idea that others enjoy it is terribly satisfying. Second, I hope, in some way, my writing might bring awareness to the vile scourge that is human trafficking. Although the story is fictional, and Peter and Zsuzsa aren't real, at least to anyone but me, if I could prevent one child from abduction, all my toil would be worth it.

I'm sure you noticed this is my first book with "The End" written at the close. Initially, I had planned to write five books in the series; however, as I wrote this one, four felt right. That doesn't mean I'm saying goodbye to Peter. I don't know if I ever could. There will be future books with Peter and Zsuzsa, and the next might just take them back to New York. I also have plans for other books with new characters. Peter will rest for a season as

I write two standalone books with new characters in new places. I plan to write both in 2024.

Thank you for buying my books. It never ceases to amaze me when I check my daily sales and see people have invested their time and resources into my stories. It means so much to me. Thank you!

D.J. Maughan

P.S. I'm offering a special bonus chapter to all those who sign up for my newsletter. Visit djmaughan.com to request your copy today.

Acknowledgements

Thank you to my series beta readers. Your insights helped shape the series. Brooke Maughan, Lupe Merino, Connie Maughan, Laurie Clark, Luke Barber, Paula Maughan, Tyler Snow, Tami Bailey, Jerry Paskett, Jim Thomas, Paul Gyorka, Tom Baugh, Mark White, Lisa Kropf, and Nate McCullouch.

A huge thank you to my editor, Jonathan Starke. Your critical feedback, positive and negative, taught me so much. I look forward to working with you for many years to come.

Made in the USA
Columbia, SC
18 December 2023

6713f845-aaa2-4447-8bd8-f621ea36f6baR01